I0580873

April Showers

Amy Laurens

Other Works

SANCTUARY SERIES
Where Shadows Rise
Through Roads Between
When Worlds Collide
The Complete Sanctuary Series

KADITEOS SERIES
How Not To Acquire A Castle

STORM FOX SERIES
A Fox Of Storms And Starlight
A Stag Of Hope And Memory

SHORTER WORKS & COLLECTIONS
April Showers
Darkness And Good
Dreaming of Forests
It All Changes Now
Of Sea Foam And Blood
Trust Issues

NON-FICTION
How To Write Dogs
How To Theme
How To Create Cultures
How To Create Life
How To Map
The 32 Worst Mistakes People Make About Dogs

Find other works by the author at
www.amylaurens.com/books

April Showers

Amy Laurens

AUSTRALIA

Copyright © 2022 Amy Laurens
2 4 6 8 10 9 7 5 3 1

All rights reserved. No part of this book may be reproduced in any form or by any electronic or mechanical means, including information storage and retrieval systems, without permission in writing from the publisher, except by a reviewer, who may quote brief passages in a review.

This is a work of fiction. All characters, organisations and events are the author's creation, or are used fictitiously.

Print ISBN: 978-1-922434-06-7
eBook ISBN: 9781393576525

www.inkprintpress.com

National Library of Australia Cataloguing-in-Publication Data
Laurens, Amy 1985—
April Showers
152 p.   cm.
ISBN: 978-1-922434-06-7
Inkprint Press, Canberra, Australia
1. Fiction—Fantasy—Contemporary 2. Fiction—Family Life—General 3. Fiction—Women 4. Fiction—Short Stories (single author)

Summary: Six rainy autumn stories about finding peace amid the trials of life.

First Edition: April 2022

Cover design © Inkprint Press.

CONTENTS

Author's Note

IN APRIL 2020, THE WHOLE WORLD CAME TO A STAND-still: Covid-19 was proving itself a deadly serious threat, challenging governments around the world to take it deadly seriously—or reap the consequences.

Australia took it seriously, a fact I am eternally grateful for, and at the very end of March, the school where I work called shut down. I was almost implausibly fortunate: combined with stringent lockdown measures that saw Australia's caseload flatten and the fact that, as a teacher, I was considered an 'essential worker', my period of actual complete lockdown was only six weeks—laughably short compared to what much of the world has had to deal with.

Nevertheless, at the time we had no way of knowing how long the school closure would last, and as part of keeping myself sane, I decided to do a writing challenge over the two weeks of the spring break. Ten stories in twenty days. It was ambitious, a NaNoWriMo of sorts, and I had no idea how or whether I'd manage it. But following Dean Wesley Smith's advice of 'failing to success', I figured I'd aim for ten-in-twenty, and be proud of whatever I ended up achieving.

What I ended up with was this anthology that you now hold in your hands: not ten-in-twenty, but six-in-fourteen, which I was still very proud of—and after which, coming on the back of two weeks of teaching online, I was ready to never see a computer screen again (or at least for a couple of weeks).

You'll see this context come through in these stories: the ideas of escape, of illness, of finding peace amidst chaos...

These are all prominent themes in this anthology.

I think these themes are enduring enough that you will find something to enjoy in these stories irrespective of your experiences with Covid-19. And I also wanted you to understand why, when the main character in the final story laments having been housebound for three weeks (Oh no! Not *three whole weeks!*), some of the stories now seem almost wondrously naïve about the nature of a global pandemic and protracted lockdowns.

Regardless, may you, too, be blessed with the ability to find moments of peace amid chaos.

Crystalline And Bright

I STOOD, STARING DOWN INTO THE TEAL-BLUE RIVER water, ignoring the chatter behind my back. Snow covered the ground around me, hiding bumps and ridges, soothing out sharp edges. To my right, the dark stone shadow of the bridge stood like a guardian, watchful, alert. Snow rimmed its edges; every so often some shifted in a sudden breeze and landed in the quiet river below with a gentle splash.

The willows on the far bank slept quietly under their snow blanket, their green sappy smell hidden by the cold, sharp scent of the snow.

Stop.

Start again.

It wasn't actually winter. It was early spring, with the grass green and new, the sound of a lawnmower buzzing in the distance and the scent of cut grass drifting on the wind. Moss covered the shadowed side of the old stone bridge, and willows stretched their fingers to the slow-moving, drowsy little river that bordered the grounds of the school.

A butterfly flittered past, white wings speckled with black like soot.

The world felt fresh, and green, and full of promise.

I was still ignoring the chattering behind me.

Stop.

Start again.

It's summer, and the air is swelteringly hot. Sweat drips down the back of my neck, pools under my arms, under my awkward breasts. The river in front of me is milky-blue, gentle, quiet, and I long to strip off my shirt and jeans and throw myself into the water.

It's not just the breathtakingly sharp cold of the icemelt I'm craving; it's the feeling of being *clean*.

The air stinks of a fish that Lander left out on the bank near the bridge, rotting to pieces in the high temperatures.

I'm still ignoring the chatter.

Stop.

Let's try once more.

It's autumn—of course—and the willows have turned yellow, their little leaves dropping into the milk-water, eddying slowly away from the shadow of the bridge.

Behind me, the emerald lawn of the old school buildings is ringed with gem-toned maples, butter-leafed poplars, silver-and-gold birches. Occasionally, the wind catches stray leaves and flings them into the pond.

I can still hear the voices behind me.

All of these pictures are true, and none of them are.

Not precisely, not uniquely; they're all composites, the merging and piecing together of hundreds of memories of similar experiences, of all the times I stood on the river bank and stared longingly into its depths, imagining myself a naiad with a secret home to return to, somewhere people loved me.

These images have to be composites, because for every time I was down at the river, I was focusing only on two things: ignoring the voices, and watching the water.

All the other details, the little bits of specificity that allow me to recall the place in so much explicit detail? I never noticed them at the time.

And so I have to piece them together, collage-fashion, or else I have nothing to say. Nothing to see.

Nothing except the water, milky-blue that occasionally, in the right light, at the right time of day, flashed teal and came alive.

I'd lived with the voices as long as I could remember. Some of them were real, inasmuch as they belonged to real, live people whom other people could see, who grew and developed and changed with the passing of the seasons; some of them were *surreal*, inasmuch as they belonged to people I could see, but that none other could, and who did not change or grow with the passing of the seasons.

And some of the voices... Some of them I could never divine exactly what they were.

But all of them, real, surreal and unknown, had one thing in common: none of them liked me.

I could never figure out why. Oh, sure, I came to the school without the name and pedigree of any of the other students, a supposed-orphan with no memory of her life before double digits and no connections to speak of. I wasn't part of their circle, my excellent trust fund notwithstanding, and so the real people, the live people, couldn't accept me.

It shouldn't have been that way. It seemed to me that I hadn't done anything wrong, or untoward, hadn't neglected to do anything needed, hadn't slighted or snubbed any who hadn't already done so several times to me.

And yet, for all the years I was there at the school, its grand, lofty double-storey buildings made from pale stone like a castle, ivy creeping all about like Christmas lights, the lawn constantly emerald, the hedges consistently clipped... For all those composite years, no one ever liked me.

Well, a slight exaggeration: my teachers liked me well enough. I was a diligent student.

And the river liked me. I could tell that, because when I was close to the river, the other voices kept their distance—and the river had a voice of its own. And once or twice, I could have sworn it also had a face.

The first time I realised that one day I would escape was a crystalline autumn evening, golden sunlight dripping through the willows, the towering ashes that bordered the school along the river behind me dappling the grass as they caught and hoarded the light. The air was still, the river was slow, and the voices, for once, reduced to only those that I alone could hear; my fellow students were, for the most part, packing their rooms away in preparation for the autumn holidays, which began at 5pm that night.

Holidays were awkward.

No one came for me, but they couldn't hold the boarding house open for a mere one student, so I was shipped off to a hotel in the city, notionally under the guardianship of the principal—to whom I had been generically entrusted at the age of ten with an anonymous trust fund large enough to secure my private education and then some—but in actually, now that I was seventeen, fending for myself.

I didn't mind so much. The voices only I could hear were quieter in the city. Not distant, like they were when I was by the river, but quieter, their constant generic disapproval of my every action diminished by all the noise of the city itself—the traffic rushing and beeping, the whirr of a thousand machines, the crowded feel of electricity and waveforms clogging up the air. All of it seemed to drain the power of my invisible voices a little, enough that they grew dim with time.

You've have thought, then, that I would have loved the city better than I did.

But for all that I spent every holidays there, roaming streets that smelled of soot and exhaust, eating strawberry gelato and margarita pizza and watching endless hours of TV, the school was still my home. When I was away, I missed the green, green grass; I missed being surrounded by trees, as though living as a dryad in a forest; and I missed the river.

And so, on this quiet, final autumn afternoon, I had come down to the river to say farewell, to listen as the wrens danced through the willows, to dip my fingers into the coolness of the water and kiss it all goodbye.

The voices stood a way behind me, back on the green, green grass of the school grounds.

In front of me, the water threw the light in a way that made it seem bottomless.

And as I stretched down to meet the water, the water stretched up to meet me.

My breath caught in my throat; for all the years I'd lived here, for all the years I'd loved the river, it had never loved me back. At least, not like this.

I swilled my fingers back and forth in the coldness, marvelling at the way the water lapped against gravity up my wrist, twining and trickling around my forearm.

The susurrus of voices behind me grew louder.

As they did, the spiralling web of water around my forearm grew stronger, gripping me with firm confidence and pulling me forward.

I had just enough time for my heart to squeeze in fear, for my breath to leave my mouth in a high-pitched squeak—and the river dragged me in, head first, the icy water shocking against the warmth of the afternoon.

I surfaced easily enough, long strands of my dark blonde hair caught in my mouth, matting over my eyes, and I trod water and scraped hair from my face and spat water that tasted slightly mineral away, and I was fine.

I scowled at the water around me. "What was that for?"

In the distance, I heard the voices laughing.

I could only be grateful, against the knot of embarrassment in my chest, that my classmates hadn't been here to witness this as well.

Around me, the water rippled, and I felt as though it laughed.

I splashed at it, trying to hold on to my irritation, my embarrassment—but in truth, the water cradled me like loving arms and I could no more be indignant at it than I could resent the sky.

I lay back, floating, sunlight sparkling on the drops of water that clung to my eyelashes. The water was cool, the sunlight was warm…

One day, not too far in the future, school would be over, and I'd be free of the anchored weight that kept me in this place.

And then a voice shouted from the shore.

"Hey, burley, your ride's here!"

I sighed, stroked for the shore, and emerged, sopping wet, by the bridge. I lifted the hem of my t-shirt, raised one foot and then the other—but the water streamed from me like I'd become the river itself, and I knew there was no point trying to dry. Deflated, I headed for the boarding house, steeling myself for the mockery I knew would greet me.

By the time I reached the foyer of the boarding house, however, a high-ceiling, dark room that smelled of must and age, there was no longer any reason for mockery: my clothes, my shoes, my hair? All perfectly dry.

I didn't understand—but I didn't have time to give it much thought. My chauffeur was here, and the matron of the boarding house clapped her big hands and shooed me upstairs to get my bags, and ten minutes later I was in the back of the sleek, black car, leaving the school grounds for a little over two weeks.

As the car pulled out onto the secluded country road that led back into town, I twisted, craning my neck for one last glimpse—not of the school, but of the river.

Surely I had imagined the river reaching up to grab me. Surely I had just overbalanced, inventing the loving caress of the river as a poor substitute for all the affection my living life lacked.

But I bit the inside of my lip and thought about the way the susurrus of voices had gotten louder, excited, as the river had reached up to me—and how even now, though I couldn't understand their words any more than I had ever been able to, the voices around me seemed electrified.

I pressed my fingers against the cool glass of the car window and daydreamed of milky-blue rivers and sparkling icemelt that winked and smiled in the sunlight.

The two weeks in the city felt endless. The weather had turned, the days short and chill, the leaves on the few extant trees turning crimson and scarlet and gold, and it made leaving my apartment difficult. Once I was out, wrapped in an ivory down jacket, my ice-blue scarf tucked about my throat, the cold wasn't so bad; it wasn't the fierce bite of winter yet, and the afternoon sun still held warmth—but it was an impediment, inertia that needed to be overcome to get out of the apartment every morning.

The holidays were a strange, timeless place in my life, without deadlines, without schedules—without any other human desire to intrude upon my own.

It had used to be lonely, but by the time of these holidays, with my eighteenth birthday tugging at my awareness—the Friday before I was due back at school—I'd acclimatised.

I hadn't always been alone. I felt certain of that. Every now and then, when I was exiting the shower or running the tap in the kitchen sink, I opened my mouth to call to someone over the noise... Only before I could speak, I remembered that I was alone, that there was no one here to call to.

In the first week of the holidays, though, just days after the river had pulled me in, I was washing my hair under a stream of hot water, steam clouding the bathroom air filled with the aroma of rose-geranium shampoo and aloe vera conditioner, and I felt it.

I stiffened, hands buried in the lathered suds of my long hair, water running hot down my back. "Hello?" It was the first time I'd actually managed to speak when that strange sensation—almost remembrance—of not being alone came over me. "Adamaris?"

Adrenalin tugged in my chest. Adamaris? I didn't remember speaking that name before, and yet somehow the shape of it was familiar in my mouth.

The shower water ran cold, cold as the icemelt river.

I shrieked, leaping to the side of the shower, out of the flow of water—but the spray from the shower followed me, twining about my body, curving over my shoulders and down my spine, spiralling around my legs, my arms.

For the first time I could remember, the voices fell completely silent.

I stood, heart pounding, until the suds from my hair dripped into my eye. I hissed at the pain and winced, shoved my face under the water to wash it… And the water ran warm once more.

The rest of the holidays passed in a blur of cosy-chaired reading and bundled-up walks, stops at the café where I got my breakfast and lunch and quiet nights illuminated by the tungsten bulbs that reflected golden in the glass of the apartment windows.

My birthday passed largely unremarked, aside from the letter from the bank declaring my trust fund to be, at last, my own, no intermediary required. I squeezed the bright blue card between my fingers and bit my lip to hide the grin.

I was so, so nearly free.

The terms of my trust fund had stipulated that I remain at the school until the age of eighteen, when the money could legally be mine, but there were no conditions attached as to what I had to do after that. Technically, I needn't even return to school for my final three terms... But it seemed silly to waste all the money that my generous, anonymous benefactor had invested into my education.

Still. I tapped the card against the tip of my nose, breathing in the sharp scent of the plastic, and grinned.

Nearly free. Nearly.

I didn't realise how nearly it was. When I woke up in the morning, my apartment was silent. For the first time I could remember, apart from that brief moment in the shower last week, the susurrus of disapproving voices was gone.

I tried out the familiar-yet-strange name on my tongue: "Adamaris?"

No one answered.

But the silence filled me with almost as much joy as any answer might have done. The voices were gone. I was free from their disapproval at last.

The day I returned to school, it was raining. Not a gentle, autumn rain that soaked the ground and raised the last crop of mushrooms before the cold of winter; no. This was a fierce gale, with raging winds driving the water almost horizontal, pushing me— and the car, and the spruce trees along the road— inevitably toward the school.

But despite the noise of the storm, for the first time, I was heading toward school in silence. The voices hadn't returned.

We pulled through the wrought-iron gates with leaves and twigs flappering madly at the car's roof and windscreen, and the chauffeur inched down a driveway barely visible through the rain and debris.

At the end of the drive, we stopped under the portico outside the boarding house foyer, and I leapt from the car, navy-blue woollen coat clutched tightly at my chin. The wind whipped my cheeks, my hair tugging to get free from the loose bun I'd tied it up in, and the chauffeur all but threw my bags on the doorstep before slamming the boot, re-entering the car, and hightailing it as fast as he could safely go away from the school, and the storm.

I stood, staring after the red taillights that gleamed like eyes in the dim light, a strange sense of grief weighing down my chest. Wind snapped at me, spitting ice-cold rain in my face, the scent of wet stone and wet grass almost taking my breath away.

I had the strangest feeling that I would never see the chauffeur again.

Snorting at my whimsy, I shook my head, collected my bags, and headed for my room.

The storm blew itself out overnight, and the morning that dawned was crystalline and bright. A soft, pale sky gleamed like a fresh-water pearl and the smell of damp grass permeated even the must of the boarding house.

Before breakfast I was outside, crossing the debris-strewn lawn briskly, the hems of my jeans growing damp as I swished toward the river.

Through the silver birches that had been stripped of nearly all their leaves overnight, under the tall, tall ashes... Something tight in my chest eased as I glimpsed the milk-blue river. In the soft morning light, it seemed deeper teal than usual, and strange currents seemed to play in it. The river was usually slow and languid, but this morning, sticks and twigs eddied and twirled in the middle, flotsam and jetsam from the night's storm washed up along a high-water line a few feet above the level of the water.

I knelt beside it anyway, water soaking through the knees of my jeans in seconds.

I should have been freezing. The air was chill and crisp, the world was damp and sleepy—and the river raced alongside me, rushing with a noise like the pouring rain, white foaming in lacy webs across its surface.

"You're in a hurry today," I murmured as I dipped my fingers into the icy flow.

It shocked me not at all when the river rippled up to meet me, bubbles and foam tracing ornamental lattices up my skin.

This time, I remembered to grab a breath before the water dragged me under. A good thing, too, because the current was even stronger than it had looked. It dragged me down, down, down, turning me, tumbling me like a rock.

I bashed against a boulder deep below the surface, crying out instinctively, grasping after the air as it left my lungs.

Tumble.

Tumble.

Which was way up?

I couldn't see the surface, couldn't hear anything but the roar of the water against my eardrums.

My lungs began to burn.

I pressed one hand over my mouth, pinching my nose. With the other, I stroked desperately, kicking out with all my strength, praying desperately that I'd find the surface.

Something brushed against me.

Too gentle for a rock, too large for a fish…

My chest contracted as I imagined what might be in the river. All those times I'd thought I'd seen an eye, a glimpse of a smile… The long, watery fingers that had reached up and pulled me in.

The creature bumped against me again, pressing against my side. My fingers caught at something that felt like hair. I clutched.

Faster than breathing, the thing I'd caught hold of raced through the water. The sudden increase in speed left my stomach somewhere at the bottom of the river—but we shattered through the surface into the sunlight and I gasped greedily at the air, scraping hair from my face, clinging at the creature that had saved me.

It nudged my cheek.

I squeezed water from my eyes, moved the last of my unruly hair—and stared into the huge, shining eye of a horse.

A horse, but it was teal and semi-transparent, made of water, white foam dripping down its neck in place of a mane, every bit as large and as real as a regular horse—only here, with me, in the stream.

It nudged at me again with its gentle nose.

My eyes were wide, my mouth open—and my fingers entwined in its mane, and it had saved me.

The water-horse snorted, sending spray over my face. I flinched, then laughed. "Adamaris?" I asked, though it didn't feel quite right.

The horse clearly knew the name, however; it pivoted instantly, encouraging me vigorously to mount. So I did, and the horse sped down the river effortlessly like a dolphin, milky-blue and white and crystal bright. The fresh, mineral tang of the water coated my lips and cold air buffeted my cheeks and the tip of my nose.

I'd never been above the bridge before—at least, not that I could remember—but there was nothing to do now but cling tightly to a horse made of water and foam and laugh as the spray from our passing glittered in the sunlight now cresting over the treetops.

High up in the mountains, the river dwindled to a stream, deep and purposeful—and cold as it passed into a crevice in the rocks, hidden from the sun. Dark rock walls narrowed to either side until I could have brushed my fingers against them with outstretched arms, had we not been travelling so fast I feared I'd injure myself if I tried.

Abruptly, my darling teal water-horse reared. It seemed that surely I should fall off—but I stayed as securely mounted as if the horse had merely drawn to a gradual halt.

My chest lightened. I breathed deeply of cold air that smelled of mineral water and mountain rock and moss.

The horse replanted its feet, tossing its head at a narrow gap in the rocks ahead, from whence this mountain river was born.

"Am I supposed to go in there?" I said, not sure what sort of answer I could expect.

But the horse tossed its head clearly enough, so I slipped from its back, heart pitter-pattering in my chest, and climbed the small, smooth boulders to the gap. Green algae slicked the rocks, slimy under my hands, but I didn't slip, and I didn't fall. The water splashing over my arms, leaping at my legs, was like ice—but I didn't feel the cold.

Instead, my heart pounded faster with strange anticipation. I scrambled through the gap, rough stone pressed on either side—and inside, in the darkness, over the rushing noise of the stream that covered me to mid-thigh, the voices returned.

Disappointment stabbed me. My jaw twitched. I hadn't missed the voices, or their constant disapproval of my life.

But... I tilted my head. Somehow, even through the noise of the stream, the voices seemed a little clearer now, as though if only the water would quiet, I might actually understand them.

Hesitant, water dripping from my hair, my eyebrows, my nose, I stepped forward.

Deep in the depths of the cave, blue light flared.

My breath caught in my chest; I forgot for a moment how to move.

But the stream that still flowed around me lapped gently, reaching up to twine around my hips and waist, a soft and gentle encouragement filled with that same sense of liking I'd always felt from it.

And so, after a deep inhale of mineral-rich air, I waded toward the light.

The rushing of the stream and the susurrus of voices drowned out my thoughts, like moving through a dream, one swishing, swirling, laboured step after another. I couldn't tell if it was a handful of minutes or an armload, but soon the light grew close.

It wasn't a light.

Well, it was, but there was more than one—and they weren't simply lights. They were people.

They were the voices.

And as I drew close, at last I could understand them.

"Ridiculous decision, sending her out like that."

"What did they think was going to happen if something went wrong?"

"Can't believe they left her with nothing but us for protection."

"They didn't *think*."

"Constantly in danger, no idea who she is…"

"…how can she even decide?"

I couldn't stand. My heart was pounding so hard it might burst out of my chest, and I couldn't stand up another moment.

I sank to the rocks at the side of the stream, the narrow cave lit only by the blue glow of these beings that glimmered and glinted off the tealy-blue water, my hand gripping tightly against the wall.

It sounded… I swallowed, blinked, shook my head.

These were the same voices that had followed me as long as I could remember. I even recognised some of the beings as the people that had haunted my vision, the ones I'd quickly learned that others couldn't see, the ones who didn't grow or change or develop.

I'd recognise their tone of disapproval anywhere. But if what I was hearing was true… it wasn't me they disapproved of.

"Adamaris?" I said, quiet, full of longing, my chest a gaping hole of amnesia.

The beings quelled at once and stared at me.

"She remembers," one murmured, the elderly woman with the long, long hair and eyes as sharp as flint.

As one, they parted.

I gasped.

The world reeled.

My fingers tightened against the rocks, seeking something stable, something steadying.

Because a woman was approaching from between the beings in blue light crystalline and bright, a real woman, not something ephemeral like the blue-glowing voices, and she was tall, and the hair that spilled from her brow in soft and gentle waves to her waist was a darkish blonde, like mine, until it melted into the water of the stream, and the ice-blue eyes that smiled at me above a gently curving mouth were my eyes that stared back at me from the mirror, and although I couldn't remember anything, I couldn't imagine how I could ever forget her. "Adamaris?" I said, and my voice trembled in the dark over the sound of the rushing stream. "Mum?"

The woman whose body ceased at the level of the water melted, collapsing toward me, enfolding me in her arms and hugging me tight against her chest. "Oh, Amberly. Oh, my darling Amberly. You made it." She kissed my hair, pushed me out to arm's length to look me over in the dim blue light, held me to her again. "Oh Amberly," she said against my wet hair. "You made it."

I wasn't cold, I realised, not because my mother's arms were wrapped around me for the first time in eight years. And not because I simply wasn't noticing the water.

I wasn't cold because my body *was* the water.

I was water, I was flesh, I was my mother's daughter—and after a long, long absence, I was home.

Love In The Time Of Corona

THUNDER RUMBLED OVERHEAD AS SARIA STOOD AT the clothesline against the northern wall of the house, but one glance and she knew there'd be no rain. There hadn't been for a month, not since the hail-storms that had heralded the start of an unseasonably hot autumn, so why would the weather change its mind and start now, vocal complaints aside? She pursed her lips and plunged her hands back into the half-empty basket of wet washing, savouring the coolness against the fierce heat of an evening that smelled dry, full of dust and concrete.

Saria hung a sock, because socks were easy to hang. They only needed one peg, which made them safe from her anxiety, which demanded she use the same colour of peg on any item requiring more than one.

Well, it was demanding that today. It hadn't in years, over a decade, not since high school. Ten, eleven, twelve...

Fourteen. It had been fourteen years, a good chunk of which involved therapy for her anxiety, since she'd last had this much trouble hanging out washing.

Saria fastened the sock to the line with an emerald plastic peg, went back for another sock, hung it with a faded blue peg, breathed deeply.

Thunder rumbled again, a sudden rush of wind racing past, fluttering the spade-shaped leaves on the ornamental pear behind her before disappearing. There was no good reason why it should raise a thrill of fear through her chest, that trailing, sparkling line of adrenalin she'd managed to forget.

It did it anyway.

Saria inhaled, reaching for calm, the scent of laundry powder and the faint, lingering traces of vinegar from the wash curling around her.

A shirt next, a soft, white cotton tee. Deftly, Saria grabbed it by the underarm seams and flipped it over the line. A faded red peg on one side.

Her jaw twitched.

The closest available peg on the line was another of the green ones. In fact, the next ten or so were green. She'd have to take two steps to the right to reach the closest red peg.

Her jaw twitched again.

Thunder complained softly, dying away into the distance.

Shoulders tense, the slightly metallic taste of her cheek on her tongue as she bit down on it, Saria took the two quick steps, snatched the red peg, and snapped it over the white shirt with a little more force than necessary.

She pressed her eyes closed tightly, left hand curled tight around the rim of the wash basket.

Heart knocking at her chest, Saria eyed the remainder of the pegs. There might be enough green ones left to hang everything…

Green pegs. Just use all the green pens. You can buy another packet tomorrow. It's going to be fine. You'll be fine, they'll be fine… Everyone's going to be fine.

Saria repeated the lie to herself as she hung the rest of the basket, emerald peg after emerald peg after emerald peg.

She ran out of them at the end, but it didn't matter: she'd left the other socks until last, socks and undies and face washers—anything that could be hung with only a single peg.

She breathed deeply and grabbed up the empty white basket. Fine. Everything was fine.

DAN WAS OUT OF TOILET PAPER. THE REALISATION came sharply as he reached for the roll in the middle of the night, pulling one, two, three squares free before—tck, tck, rattle—the empty cardboard tube spun fruitlessly on the holder.

He groped around on the floor for the plastic packaging that held his spare rolls—he vaguely understood that some people took them out of the plastic and stacked them neatly in corners and such, and he always aspired to such things, even if they never actually eventuated—but there was naught but crinkling, crackling plastic to meet his fingers.

Despite the heat of the previous afternoon, the early hours of the morning had cooled markedly, and the air drifting in from the open bathroom window raised goosebumps over his back. Well, shit.

Dan snorted at his terrible pun, made the best of what he had, and went back to bed, hands scented with the soft, lingering aroma of the sandalwood soap. He paused briefly to unlock his phone, squinting at the sudden bright light on his face, and left himself a reminder to hunt down toilet paper in the morning.

Talk about poor timing.

He drifted back to sleep, dreaming of cardboard tubes and empty shelves.

IT WOULDN'T HAVE BEEN SO BAD, PERHAPS, IF SARIA had been stuck in lockdown in a house with other people. But marooned in a two-bedroom townhouse alone, she had nothing to distract her from the thoughts rattling around in her head. And none of her friends or family lived close by; there was no one she could accidentally bump into at the corner store for a bit of much-needed socialisation, no one she could even walk around the block with, exercising while maintaining the strict 'no gatherings of more than two people' rule.

Her sister phoned every second day, her mother twice a week—but it wasn't the same.

It didn't keep the anxiety at bay.

She'd started sleeping with the hallway light on, to be honest. Started jumping at shadows in the dark again, every step toward the bathroom at night a torturous journey of fear clutching at her chest, her breath catching in her throat as the back of her neck prickled with the sense of being stared at.

Morning wasn't much better, these days. Even though it didn't matter in the slightest what she wore—she kept a couple of good blouses by the computer to throw on for zoom meetings and amused herself wondering how many of her colleagues were wearing pyjama pants—the decision of which shirt to put on was turning once more into an agony of indecision.

The blue one? The navy?

The brunette princess in the golden ballgown reading a huge book in an amazing library, or the unicorns with the scarves?

Saria sighed and snagged the unicorn one from the top of the washing pile, wrinkling her nose at the smell of day-old sweat as she pulled it on.

Even that didn't matter these days. No one could get close enough to smell her anyway, and the shirt calmed her down a little.

A liberal spray of rose-scented perfume sweetened the deal, and then she was trotting down the stairs, snagging her wallet off the desk, and slipping into her ballet flats for a quick walk down to the corner store.

The therapist years ago had pointed out that sometimes, the best way to win a battle was to avoid it altogether: if Saria only had green pegs, the anxiety couldn't complain about how she hung her clothes on the line.

(It would probably find another outlet, dealing with it was like playing a protracted game of whack-a-mole, but she'd take the relief where she could find it.)

Outside, she immediately regretted the unicorn shirt decision. Or, not so much that decision specifically as the implicit trust she'd placed in the weather, and the assumption that she wouldn't need her hoodie.

Alack, the weather had betrayed her: the afternoons had been summer-hot the last few weeks, but the nights had been autumn-cold, and this morning it seemed like autumn was finally here to stay.

She inhaled deeply, and the cold air sent long-clawed fingers down to seize her lungs. Urgh. It smelled like rain, and goosebumps prickled up and down her arms. Better walk quickly.

DAN WOKE TO HIS PHONE ALARM BLARING, DRAGGED forcibly to consciousness. He dressed in a daze, vaguely aware somewhere that staying up late every night watching B-grade movies and ordering pizza was going to catch up with him eventually.

With his wallet, if nothing else, because home-delivered pizza wasn't the cheapest meal, and the café he'd bought two years ago when he'd moved to Canberra couldn't sustain its business with only take-away orders. He had enough savings to last him awhile, he was lucky in that regard, but his next pay cheque wouldn't be coming in until the end of April when the government welfare payments kicked in.

He paused at the front door of his townhouse, cold morning air drifting over him. That storm front yesterday had done a number on the weather; autumn was apparently here.

Dan snatch up his dark green beanie and crammed it over his loose curls—he'd usually cut them when they got this long, but where was he going to go for the next few months except the grocery store and the government shopfront, and no one at either of those would care about the length of his hair.

These musings took him the first of the three blocks to the tiny shopping complex that served the suburb, and recalculating exactly how long he could make his savings last entertained him the rest of the way.

He had enough money, really. He wasn't in danger of losing his townhouse, wasn't in danger of not being able to eat. He wasn't in the high-risk group for the virus, didn't have any personal contacts who were.

Didn't have many personal contacts at all, really. And that was the point, the thing he kept circling around, working desperately to avoid thinking about. Because the one thing—the only thing—he was in danger of really was loneliness.

Two years, working long hours and weekends to establish the cafe and get it running, playing around writing scripts on the side—because that was what he *really* wanted to do with his life—all of it left him with precious little time to establish any local friendships.

Not that locality mattered any more these days anyway.

Dan entered the small grocery store, the distinctive scent of the air-conditioned air greeting him as he squirted sanitiser on his hands and rubbed it in.

It was tempting to browse, to see if there was anything else he could distract himself with, but he ought to be careful with his money and anyway, toilet paper was a precious commodity and a small distraction might cost him his opportunity.

Sure enough, in the last aisle to the right, opposite the four freezer doors that encased the ice creams and frozen yogurts and sorbets, the toilet paper shelves were empty.

Except...

Dan felt a tiny seed of relief.

One last packet, eight rolls of three-ply, tucked to the side down on the bottom shelf.

Dan took a step closer—

And a woman, shortish, with shiny chocolate-brown hair and a terribly cute grey shirt with four be-scarved unicorns on it crouched down and beat him to it.

His instinct was to lunge at the toilet paper packet. He was out, completely and utterly out and what was he supposed to do? Use a sponge like he was an ancient Roman or something?

The woman glanced up, caught his eye—and something fountained through his chest because holy *shit* she was beautiful—and she was holding the last pack of toilet paper.

Urgh.

"Oh," she said, straightening. "Were you after this too?"

He nodded wordlessly. Something around the corners of her eyes was tight, something in the set of her shoulders—but if she hadn't been holding the last pack of toilet paper, his pack, the packet he really, really needed, he might have stopped breathing there and then.

"I don't even need it, really," she said, eyes over-wide, and he realised the tips of her fingers had blushed white as she gripped the package.

Somehow, it lessened his frustration, and he took half a step back.

"I don't need it," she whispered again, voice thick with misery... No, something deeper than that. Grief.

Despite himself, Dan's brow wrinkled. "Are you sure?" Because people didn't usually sound like they were grieving at the thought of giving up a few rolls of toilet paper, the absurd situation the world was in right now notwithstanding.

Wordlessly, the woman offered him the package, the plastic crinkling as she held it out to him, gaze averted.

Cautiously, he reached for it. "Normally I wouldn't," he said slowly, to match his gesture. He had the feeling that if he moved too fast right now, she'd spook—and somehow, he didn't want that. "But I really am completely out."

She glanced up at him, a sparkle lurking in her rich brown eyes despite their tightness. "Really?"

Dan nodded. A self-deprecating smile. "Yeah. Ran out right in the middle of the night, too. Super inconvenient." Why was he telling her this? No one, let alone a strange woman in the grocery store, wanted to hear about his toilet paper misadventures. It took everything he had not to wince.

Her lips quirked, an adorable, deep dimple springing to life in her cheek. "You'd better take it then. I have plenty, really."

The relief he felt as she relinquished the package to him was palpable; he breathed easier, his shoulders relaxing as he stood straighter.

She noticed, and a sparkling smile emerged like the sun appearing from behind a cloud.

"So, how many rolls *do* you have?" His mouth had developed a weird kind of sentience of its own, because he would never say something that stupid if he was actually thinking.

But the woman grinned, eyes crinkling adorably. "Twenty-three."

Dan raised his eyebrows. "That's a very precise number."

"I'm a very precise person," she said, still grinning. "Are you really actually out?"

He nodded, a twinge in his stomach.

The woman laughed, and if he'd thought the sun came out before, it was nothing to this. Her laugh was utterly un-self-conscious—utterly infectious. He found himself grinning along, tracing the lines of her mouth with his eyes.

She had great teeth. One of the top ones on the right, first one in from the canine, was a little crooked, but it gave her an adorable air of mischief as she laughed—at him, with him, it didn't matter.

"How on earth did you let yourself run out in a situation like this?" she said, twirling her fingers in the air at the world in general.

A few strands of her long, chocolate-brown hair had fallen over her face, and he found himself longing to reach out and brush it aside.

"I refused to buy in to the panic," Dan said. Brushing his fingers against her face would have been inappropriate even in normal situations, let alone now when it would so flagrantly violate the one-point-five-metres rule.

She nodded along like she knew what he was thinking, shifting her packet of green pegs in the crook of her elbow, the packet crinkling. "You refused to panic buy—which, okay, good on you, I wish I had that kind of self-restraint—only you left it too late and now there's none to be had for love or money, is that it?"

Dan nodded as they effortlessly sidestepped together, making room for a mid-forties man in a suit just on the blue side of navy who came shambling down the aisle, wrapped in a cloud of oblivion and cheap men's cologne, the kind that got into your throat if you breathed too deeply. Dan worked his tongue to clear the taste.

"You know one of the supermarkets in Belconnen has given up entirely?" the woman said, eyes tracking the blue-suited man as he headed back toward the milk. She glanced up and met Dan's gaze briefly, and something warm zipped through him. "Their toilet paper aisle is just full of nappies."

Dan's eyebrows rose. "Well, that's one solution I guess."

A pause, then she snorted in amusement. "Guess so."

A crack of thunder interrupted the conversation. Dan glanced around, surprised to note that the store did seem to have grown dim, the fluorescent lights taking on the kind of brightness they only got when robbed of daylight.

Dammit. Oh well. At least the toilet paper came in a plastic wrapping. It would get home dry and unharmed, even if he didn't.

The sudden realisation that the lovely woman with the pegs was breathing fast hit him, and he refocused on her. "Hey, are you okay?"

"Yeah, I just walked up is all," she said, and threw him a strained smile. "Hope it doesn't rain." Abruptly, she turned and headed for the cash registers at the front of the store.

He followed, because he needed to pay for his toilet paper—and definitely not because she looked worried, seemed unsettled all of a sudden, and he wanted to make sure she was okay.

Flirting in the toilet paper aisle. Saria shook her head. Had you ever heard of anything more ridiculous?

Still, she couldn't *quite* conceal the little smile that begged to be let out through her pursed lips as the man with the toilet paper—The Man With The Toilet Paper—joined the queue behind her, standing, like her, on his allotted white square, the ones management had taped to the floor, bearing the words "Queue 1.5m Apart".

Usually, Saria would be disappointed at herself for giving in, yet again, to her burgeoning anxiety and visiting the toilet paper aisle at all. Twenty-three rolls was more than enough to last her, the single occupant of her house, for several weeks, if not more.

(It occurred to her that she didn't actually *know* how long it took her to go through a packet of toilet paper, and the anxiety reared its head: these days, that seemed like a crucial detail to be aware of. She'd have to create a calendar tracker or something.)

Saria shook her head firmly, disguising it to any watching eyes as a way to toss her hair from her shoulders. Enough. She had the pegs, that would avoid that outlet. She was a grown woman and there was no one else in the house to complain if she wandered around with lights on a nighttime, even for a brief trip to the bathroom (even if it did feel like losing, most nights). And everyone in the world was supposed to be washing their hands continuously these days, so even if that *had* been the key factor that had unburied the anxiety she'd worked long years to make peace with, it was, in these days, an utter necessity. But she wasn't going to beat herself up about the toilet paper.

Struck by the sudden reminder that she hadn't cleaned her hands since she'd used the sanitiser at the entrance of the store, Saria shifted uncomfortably on her square. Her hands felt too dry, too large—too unclean, covered with whatever invisible filth she might have picked up by touching things in the store.

To be fair, she'd only touched the peg packet and the toilet paper, though so had the man... But no, she'd given *him* the package, he was bearing *her* germs and not the other way around.

Saria glanced behind her to where the man who, even at a distance of one-point-five metres, carried the faint scent of soap and something creamy that reminded her of vanilla, but softer, more subtle. It was, she had to admit, an extremely comforting smell.

And something about the way his long, strong fingers danced around the handle of the black shopping basket, the way his brown hair curled out from under the hunter-green beanie—he'd been sensible enough to check the weather before he left, unlike her—the soft, dark growth of hair over his cheeks and strong, slightly concave chin that was either three days of refusing to shave or else a carefully manicured short beard, she couldn't quite tell...

Saria's lips twitched. He was watching her.

He'd glanced away as soon as she'd looked at him, fast enough that she couldn't prove it was her he'd been looking at—but the air of studied nonchalance as he thoroughly inspected the little fridge of flavoured milks that stood by one of the registers radiating cold and humming gently... It gave him away.

Saria grinned. "Thirsty?"

He glanced at her, eyebrows shooting up again—it was pretty cute, the way they seemed to do that whenever he was surprised or amused—but expression carefully blank. "Sorry?"

She tilted her head toward the fridge. "Thirsty?"

He blushed.

Heaven help him, he actually blushed.

Saria couldn't help it; her grin widened.

Thunder rolled, interrupting, and her happy moment was quenched as suddenly as the downpour that started outside. She frowned at the view beyond the automatic glass doors of the shop's entrance as heavy, fat raindrops splattered onto the concrete. The ground was drenched in seconds, not a dry corner left beyond the eaves of the building.

Anxiety palpated at her heart.

It's okay, she told herself through clenched jaw. *There's plenty of air circulating in here, you can wait it out for a bit without getting sick. It's going to be fine.* She fumbled for her phone in her pocket, pulling up the BOM site to check the rain radar.

"How's it looking?" the cute man said, somehow managing to peer over her shoulder without getting any closer.

Saria flashed the screen at him: a broad band of red and yellow moving east, large patches of blue and white following in its wake.

"Urgh. Good for the farmers," he said, "but I guess we'll be stuck here while it passes."

Saria's jaw twitched again.

The person in front of her moved up to the next square in line.

Saria followed suit, and the man moved up behind her too.

The rain gushed down, pounding the roof, white noise turned up to fifty. Her stomach was knotting, her grip on the pegs too tight. Stupid, to have risked coming out to get them. She should have stayed home. Pegs weren't really urgent or essential, anyway. Maybe this was just punishment for bending the rules.

If she'd stayed home this morning, she would have gone nuts.

More nuts, she amended.

But being stuck in the smallish grocery store for an hour while the rain passed wasn't exactly going to be good for her mental health either. There was only one door. Not everyone was using the hand sanitiser provided as they walked in. There was nowhere clean to sit, nowhere that wasn't risking exposure, risking her mother's health...

Saria pressed her eyes closed tightly. *It's fine. I'll get Hannah to check in on Mum for the next fourteen days, just to be safe. They have air-conditioning in here, the air's being cycled through.*

They probably don't have medical-grade filters.

There aren't that many people here anyway, maybe twenty, thirty of us in the whole store including employees. Just keep your distance, have a shower and change your clothes when you get home.

You'll be fine. Mum'll be fine.

Cute Hat Guy—Shoot, when had she given him a moniker? Did she really feel that much of a spark between them, or was she just that starved for human company?—cleared his throat gently behind her.

Saria glanced around, realised the person in front of her had finished paying for their goods, stepped forward and laid her pack of pegs on the counter with a crinkle diminished by the roaring of the downpour on the roof.

Her chest was tight, and it was impossible to tell if it was asthma or anxiety—or covid, obviously, but that was a long shot option.

Her anxiety reminded her it *was* still an option, though, as she tapped her bank card on the pay terminal, declined a receipt, and re-collected her pegs sans shopping bag.

She went to the glass doors mostly out of habit, and stood for a long moment watching the rain fall. There were already some small puddles, there in the corner of the square of fake grass, over there by the bike rack out front of the take-away store, and along the edge of the path by the restaurant in the corner, its clear plastic awning drawn tightly closed, the upturned chairs inside made ghostly by the combination of rain and awning.

Garlic bread. Abruptly, she was craving garlic bread.

"What are you going to do?" Cute Hat Man had joined her at the doors—'joined her' in the loose, one-point-five-metre sense of the world these days.

Saria shrugged. "I'm not really dressed for it." She could stick under the awning around the side of the little shopping complex—to the left, it joined up with the take-away store, and if she turned left again it ran down past the hairdresser and the beauty parlour, all the way to the café—but after that? Her shirt would be soaked through before she crossed the first road. And it was four blocks to home.

And, she added with a shiver as one of them stepped a little too close to the automatic doors and they shushed open, letting in a blast of frigid air, it was freezing. Goosebumps rose immediately on her bare arms. She cuddled the packet of pegs to her so that she could rub at her biceps.

If she ran home in the rain, she'd be soaked and frozen and would probably at the very least end up with an asthma attack from the cold, damp air.

If she stayed here, her anxiety would spiral. But her chances of catching anything—*logically*—were very small.

Cute Hat Man was eyeing her up, a considering sort of weight in his gaze.

He leaned forward to peer through the glass doors—they opened again, admitting another blast of chilled air that made the air-conditioning inside the grocery store seem positively cosy—and glanced back at her. "We're not supposed to linger anywhere else," he said, somewhat inexplicably.

What did he expect her to do? Was he judging her for choosing to stay here and weather out the storm rather than running home in the rain?

His tone didn't seem quite right for that, but…

"I'll be back," he said, and he ducked outside.

Saria blinked.

The large bottle of clear hand sanitiser on its stand by the doors caught her eye. Sighing, she took the single step toward it, used the edge of her hand to squirt some into one palm, and rubbed it liberally over her hands.

A couple of other customers finished paying for their goods and hovered uncertainly around the entrance nearby.

Too nearby.

There were three others, four, five…

And then the oblivious man in his almost-navy suit and 1950s slicked-back hairdo rambled through the middle of all of them, unconscious or uncaring about everyone shifting to make room for him, and stopped right in front of the glass doors so they opened and stayed that way while he surveyed the outdoors.

Saria's chest was getting tighter. She gulped at the air, but couldn't get it all the way down to the bottom of her lungs, couldn't quite catch her breath, like she was breathing through a heavy woollen blanket. The cold scent of wet concrete and moist air funnelled down her throat, stinging, biting, and that hand full of long claws seized in her lungs again.

She coughed, took a few steps away from the doors, clutched at the unsealed wooden edge of the stand that held the on-sale fruit and veggies. She closed her eyes, inhaling slowly, evenly. The tomato-scented air still didn't reach the bottom of her lungs, but that didn't matter, she wouldn't suffocate, this had happened thousands of times before and she'd never died from it yet, never passed out from lack of oxygen, everything was fine, it was all fine, she was going to be okay.

"Hey," a soft, male voice said. "Are you okay?"

Cute Hat Man, eyes full of concern, body angled toward her while keeping his distance. In his hands, two silver loaves, long and thin. Garlic bread, from the take-away.

"Yeah," Saria said tightly. "Just…"

Which was it? Too many people? Being stuck here because of the rain?

The suited man—gone, now, she realised, of course he hadn't walked to the store in his suit like that, he must have decided a brief foray into the rain was worth it to get back to his Lexus or Audi or something so he could go straight home rather than being stuck here with the riffraff—the suited man had been a trigger, but these days, that wasn't saying much.

These days, hanging laundry with mismatching pegs could set her off.

Saria sighed, tried to offer this kind, concerned stranger a smile. "I'm okay," she said. "Just an anxiety attack."

Crap. She hadn't meant to admit to that. She watched for the light in his eyes to dim like it often did when she confessed her dirty secret to people—but his expression just softened.

"Here," he said, offering one of his silver loaves to her. "You seemed cold."

Unbelievable. She hadn't voiced her desire for garlic bread, had she, when she'd stood by the door a few minutes ago? She was sure she hadn't. "You really didn't have to do that," she said as the sharp, savoury scent twined around her.

He smiled, and it was just a little shy. "You seemed cold," he said again, jiggling the foil-wrapped gift at her.

Her breath was stuck in her throat—and not, for once, because of asthma or anxiety. Heart pitter-pattering, Saria reached for the little loaf, so warm in her fingers, nestled in its armour of wrinkled foil. "Thank you," she breathed.

Another couple of shoppers finished paying for their groceries and joined the burgeoning crowd at the door.

Saria side eyed them, took half a step away.

"Come on," said Cute Hat Man. "Let's head down the back, I think there was a pallet of canned corn they might not mind us perching on."

Saria followed after him, if only to get away from the people by the front door. "What's your name?" she asked as she debated the merits of breaking open the garlic bread loaf. (Pro: Garlic bread. Delicious. Con: She hadn't washed her hands.)

"Dan. You?"

She'd sanitised. Her anxiety would just have to live with that. "Saria."

He glanced back at her. "Beautiful."

Her breath caught. She wasn't sure if he meant her name—or her. Either way, a little frisson ran through her, trailing and sparking in the same way anxiety did—but this time, entirely pleasant.

"So why pegs?" Dan asked as he led Saria to the back corner of the store, away from the rain, away from the people that had seemed to trigger her panic. Oh, bugger. "Wait, don't answer that. You don't need to answer that," he said hurriedly as they reached the pallet of corn. The last thing he wanted to do was make her more anxious.

"It's okay," she said quietly as she inspected the pallet. "It's the anxiety." She flicked him a quick sideways glance. "It's been okay for years, manageable at least, but all this..." She did that hand twirl again that she'd done earlier. "It's flaring up. Washing my hands all the time started it, I think. It's too close to the kinds of symptoms I used to have when I was younger anyway." Saria sat on the pallet with a heavy sigh. "It's stupid. Really stupid," she added with an apologetic look.

He sat as beside her as he could. "I'm not judging," he said, and unwrapped the end of his garlic bread, both because it was the obvious thing to do and so it didn't seem like he was focusing on her too much.

"I can't hang clothes out with different coloured pegs," she said, tossing her head like she either expected him to criticise her for it, or because she was already criticising herself. Following his lead, she unwrapped her loaf of garlic bread, pulled off the crust, and stuffed it into her mouth.

"That sucks," Dan said, his own crust poised halfway to his mouth, the thick, melty butter dripping down his index finger.

One of his best mates in high school had had anxiety, badly. A couple of times it had been touch and go, and Dan still occasionally had nightmares about the time Matt had had an anxiety attack right before an exam in their senior year.

They'd been seventeen, and Dan had never witnessed anything so scary in his life up till that point.

He frowned, remembering how shy Matt had been around strangers. "You don't seem like the kind of person who'd have anxiety." He shoved the crust in his mouth, then turned to Saria, wide-eyed. "Sorry, I didn't mean like I don't believe you or anything, that wasn't what I—"

"It's fine," she cut in, cradling her garlic bread in her lap. "I know what you mean. A lot of people assume anxiety means social anxiety, and yet I talk to strangers just fine." She raised her loaf at him, a kind of salute. "People don't make me anxious. I like people. It's my own thoughts that send me spiralling." She tapped a finger to the side of her forehead.

Dan felt his eyebrows tighten. "But just now, at the front..." He tilted his head toward the front of the shop.

Saria smiled wryly. "It's not the people. It's corona."

"Ah." He gave a slow nod. Rustled in his foil for another piece of garlic bread, tore it in half, popped the soft, pillowy top part of the slice into his mouth. Mmm. Best decision of the week.

Second best, maybe. Talking to Saria had surely been the first, though if he hadn't gotten the garlic bread he wouldn't have got to talk to her as much, so. A tie, maybe.

"How did you know I was craving garlic bread?" Saria asked, and he realised she was nearly halfway through her loaf.

Dan's eyebrows lifted. "I didn't. But you really did look freezing, and you seemed... tense. I, uh." The sentence stuttered to a halt. *I what? I wanted to make you smile again? I wanted to make you feel better?* None of those were normal, acceptable things to say to a woman you'd literally just met in the toilet paper aisle of the local grocery store.

She smiled though. Not a tight, self-deprecating one, or that sparkling, teasing grin like she'd given him before. This was a gentle, warm expression. Made him feel like she approved of him, like he was the best human alive, just for a second, just for now.

"You know," he said. "Under normal circumstances, I might ask you out on a date after this."

Saria grinned, that infectious, sparkling one she'd given him earlier. "Under normal circumstances, I might have agreed."

Dan shifted on the pallet, angling himself a little more toward her. "So what? We appreciate this for what it was and let it go?" *I could ask for her phone number. Would that be too much?* He couldn't bear the thought of scaring her off, even loneliness was better than that.

Saria shook her head. "Don't be ridiculous. I'm lonely as heck these days and the anxiety spirals just make it worse. Here, I'll give you my number."

Just like that.

He was floating.

"Also," she said, "I usually come here on Thursday mornings." Eyes alight with mischief, she popped a slice of garlic bread into her mouth, licking the tip of her finger.

Dan's heart double-timed. "I've never dated from two meters away before."

She shrugged. "Has anyone?"

True.

And Saria was getting out her phone, her deliciously pink tongue tip licking garlic butter away from the corner of her mouth, and she gave him her number, and he gave her his, and despite the prohibition on social gatherings, they were in the grocery store so it was all okay, and they finished their garlic bread and laughed and swapped isolation stories, and the rain gifted them the very best half hour he could have dared to imagine.

And afterwards, he went home with his toilet paper and she went home with her pegs and they both went home with a promise to call each other tomorrow. And as they reached the place where they had to turn their separate ways, a triangle of blue sky snagged on the trees in the west, and a beam of sunlight filtered down.

Moon And Morning

It was nearly dark, that moment when the trees become nothing more than black silhouettes clawing at the orange western sky, all jag-fingered and blade-leafed, when the breeze drops to nothing as the world holds its breath, pausing to appreciate the beauty of the death of another day, the end of one day's way of life.

Around me, the crowd failed to notice. Oh, sure, a few people here and there pointed or gestured from their red tartan picnic rugs or shaded their eyes to watch from their navy blue blankets while they continued the conversation with the people around them; and a whole bunch of people had their phones out, snapping a few pics of the heavenly fire before swiping, cropping, colour-adjusting, filtering, and posting to their social media. The crowd saw the sunset, but they didn't notice it.

If they had, they'd have stopped with their breath similarly held as the world plunged into sleep.

I stopped. I noticed. But then, it was kind of my self-appointed job to notice things like that.

And, I don't know, I was a morning person.

I had nothing against night-owls—I was kind of jealous of them, to be honest, given as a teenager I was supposed to be one—but it seemed to me that people who were awake to see the very beginning of every new day, who were awake and about their lives while most of the world slumbered... We were used to seeing things that other people missed.

And I was used to noticing things alone.

I sighed, and contemplated writing that down; it would have made a good start to the next chapter of my story.

Once, just once, I thought about how great it would be to not feel like such a freak (unicorn, sorry Dad) in my massive, noisy, sprawling extended family, who spread out now on the five, six, seven or so picnic mats around me anticipating both the annual fireworks, and a subsequent lunar eclipse.

The last curve of sun disappeared behind the mountains, and a moment later the breeze returned, bringing with it the scent of plastic hotdogs and chemical popcorn and all that other standard outdoor sideshow fare, designed for optimal smell and minimum cost, about as real and edible as the notebook covering my crossed legs.

Actually, I'd rather eat the notebook. Sure, the paper's bleached, but at least there's some nondigestible fibre there that's bound to be good for something.

Goosebumps prickled my skin and I rubbed them away, my calves first, then my forearms under the sleeves of my hoodie. It wasn't *cold*, not this early in the year, but the breeze post-sunset was a marked contrast to the earlier warm breaths of the day.

"There!" Someone in the throng nearby shouted, and as one, we swivelled our heads, following their outstretched arm.

Sure enough, on the flat, eastern horizon even more broken by jagged trees than the western, the moon was rising, huge and full, pale silver in the dimming twilight.

Excitement thrilled through me. The last time there'd been a full lunar eclipse with good viewing possibilities, I'd been two. I remembered approximately as much of it as you'd expect from your average two-year-old: a vague sense of sitting on my father's shoulders, curled around his warm head, his dark hair curling through my fingers; a sense of buoyancy, expectant waiting, delight.

But that could have been any one of a hundred shoulder rides, so it hardly counted.

My notebook shifted on my lap. I glanced up as a tall boy brushed past, trying hard not to disturb people as he wove his way through the picnic mats but—hello, my notebook—failing. "You right?" I said, meaning 'are you alright', wanting to make sure he wasn't going to lose his footing and tumble on top of someone or something.

He pulled a face down at me that I could barely discern in the growing dark, one eyebrow raised in disbelief or disdain or dis-something. "Sorry," he said in that tone that meant he thought I was the one who should be sorry, and kept moving.

"No, I—" I sighed. Too late. He'd already moved on, wending his way past one of our peripheral mats where three of my young cousins hooted with laughter as their dad snapped a pack of neon glowsticks.

Pity. From this angle, in bad lighting, he'd been kind of cute.

The moon began climbing its long arc toward the zenith, and the buzz in the crowd grew. I stretched my legs out in front of me and wriggled my toes, pleased that I'd remembered to pack socks. Early autumn afternoons were t-shirt and shorts weather, but after dark with that bit of a breeze, socks and a hoodie were necessary for comfort.

Beside me, my little brother glanced up. "How long?"

He was the one in our family doing phone service, playing merge-the-dragon or whatever it was he was currently into. I guess I didn't blame him. He was nine, old enough that sitting on the family rug all night was boring, too young to be trusted to wander around in the dark like the older kids, and there was no one in our rather significant extended family around his age. Mum called him a happy accident, born seven years after me, ten years after my older brother. I mostly just called him a brat.

"Um, I think the fireworks are at eight," I said, crossing my ankles, sticking off the mat on the cold, dark grass.

My notebook slipped and I snatched it.

"Why'd you even bring it?" Harry said. "It's dark."

"Shut up," I said reflexively. He was right, obviously, but it was... I don't know, kind of a comfort blanket or something. I hated going anywhere without a notebook and pen. You never knew when inspiration was going to strike, and I'd never forgiven myself for that one time I'd come up with a whole story sequence for my latest fanfic while out grocery shopping with Mum a few years ago—which I'd of course completely forgotten by the time I'd arrived back home.

I leaned back on my elbows and breathed deeply of the cool, popcorn-scented air. Half an hour till the fireworks, then another hour until the start of the eclipse at nine. The weekend couldn't get much better than this.

Twenty minutes later, I was regretting my earlier optimism. A small horde of tiny children had gone rushing past, literally stepping all over my legs; I'd put my elbow in the remains of the hummus dip and now my hoodie sleeve was wet and cold from trying to clean it; and my cousin Ben, age four, had upended his lemonade on my notebook during the three minutes it was off my lap during the hummus episode.

And then, to make things even more exciting, Mum's phone rang. I mean, that's not the exciting bit per se, but it *was* pretty unusual; the phone waves or whatever they were got really, really clogged during Skyfire every year, and getting anything more than a basic text through was practically a miracle.

This was a really, really good moment for a miracle. It was Aunt Izzy. Luna was missing.

Now, a word of explanation about Luna and Aunt Izzy. Luna is two, just about the cutest two-year-old in the whole wide world if you ask me—which people frequently did, since I was Aunt Izzy's number one babysitter of choice—with her gleaming, golden hair and cute little snub nose and huge hazel eyes.

And yes, she's named after *that* Luna, because my Aunt Izzy is one of those Millennials who grew up with a certain scarred orphan boy they all knew and loved, and her son's name is Ron and they have a pair of dogs called Draco and Sirius, and honestly, I don't even understand how she found a husband who let her get away with all that, but hey. I write fanfic for lols and funsies, so I'm not exactly judging.

And I was especially not judging right now, with a scant ten minutes to the fireworks and a two-year-old missing in the darkness.

Aunt Izzy had gone up to the hot dog vendor to grab a snack for Ron (age six) and Luna had gone with them. Aunt Izzy had let go of Luna's hand for, like, twenty seconds to pay for the hot dog and retrieve her change, and when she reached down again, Luna was gone.

She was frantic (understandably). Had Luna made it back to us? Could we see her anywhere?

We all stood up and peered around, but trying to find a small child in a thick crowd in the dimming twilight was a losing proposition.

"We should split up," I said, frowning. Poor little Luna baby, lost in the crowd and the dark. "Take an area each and meet back here when the fireworks go off."

"Good idea, Rory," Mum said. "You head up that way along the path. Ed," she continued, pointing to my dad, "you take the inland bit there, and I'll go this way. Izzy can take the last quadrant. Harry," she said sternly, frowning down at him. "You sit here on your phone and you *do not move*, do you understand me?"

He sighed audibly, but nodded.

"Not even for the bathroom. I mean it."

"Yes, Mum."

I wound my way down the slight slope toward the footpath, then took off, heading southeast along the shore of the lake.

Every few steps I had to stop or dodge off onto the grass as another knot of people wandered by, talking loudly, laughing and shouting and squealing in the ensuing night. Ahead of me, the moon no long looked quite so fat, but it was blazingly bright and clear.

Bats flew by silently, fruit bats that lived in the parkland that edged the lake, their silhouettes crisp and classically batty against the moon.

Any other night, I'd have been delighted to see them. Now, though, they just seemed like a bad omen, even though they couldn't really be an omen for anything seeing as this was where they lived and this was the time of night they awoke.

Urgh.

Trees—mostly gnarled eucalypts—began to encroach on the slope of the lawn that led down to the lake, and the crowd thinned. From this distance, the scent of popcorn and hot chips was just a memory; here, the smell of the lake water itself was stronger, cold and algae-ish.

My heart clenched.

Surely there were enough people around that if an unsupervised two-year-old fell in the lake, someone would fish her out...

Surely.

I sped up to a jog, my eyes roving not just the grass on either side of the path now, but the edges of the lake as well.

If it had been a natural lake it might have been okay; there would have been gentle shallows, a gradual increase in depth. But this was a manmade lake, and while I'd heard it wasn't *that* deep throughout, it didn't have to be deep to drown a two-year-old—and the drop-off was immediate, and unrailled.

I could hear my breath, feel it catching in my throat. That cold spot on my elbow burned. But it would be nothing if I couldn't find Luna. I sped into a run.

Please be okay, please be okay.

It wasn't just that I was her primary non-parental babysitter. Our family had a *lot* of cousins, even a cluster of them around my age. But I was the only girl. At least, I had been until two years ago, when little Luna had come along.

She wasn't just my cousin. She was practically my sister.

Hold on, Luna. I'm coming.

There was a small service road running parallel to the footpath on my left now, spindly trees and bulbous shrubs dark, irregular shapes in the night. The crowd sounded far, far away, even though I'd only been running for a couple of minutes, and although the odd couple or cluster of people sat on the edge of the water waiting for the fireworks to start, I had the footpath to myself.

Surely I'd come too far. She was two, and Aunt Izzy had called us within minutes of her disappearing. There was no way she could have beat me all the way down here.

And my side was starting to grab. When I'd eaten a giant box of popcorn in addition to the veritable mountain of cheese and fruit and crackers and dips and chocolate we'd brought to the picnic, I hadn't been planning on having to run less than an hour later.

I stopped, gasping heavily, fingers laced together and leaning on one thigh.

Someone else would have found her. They had to have.

I turned around—and smacked straight into someone's chest. I drew in a flustered gasp that tasted like cinnamon doughnuts and tried to detangle myself—but I stepped left and so did he, and then we both stepped right, and for a second it was a mess of flailing limbs and disaster.

"Sorry!" I squeaked as we finally disengaged—and my cheeks went hot in the dark.

It was the boy, the one who'd knocked my notebook in my lap earlier.

My heart thudded.

He wouldn't remember me.

He couldn't remember me. He hadn't even looked at me, there was no reason for him to remember me.

"What, no precious notebook?"

He remembered me.

Oh, no, he remembered me, and he thought I'd been snarky at him, and I didn't have time to stop and set him straight because Luna, and the fireworks were about to start, and someone else had to have found her, they had to have.

I sidestepped him and ran, northwest back toward the crowd, my picnic rug, and safety.

Someone else had found her. Aunt Izzy, in fact. Luna had been wandering through the little vendors-only carpark that backed the food caravans, heading up the gentle slope toward the main road, chattering happily to herself in mostly-incomprehensible baby babble about the moon.

I reached the family's blue tartan picnic rug right as the first fireworks exploded in the air, a glittering shower of gold and orange and pink that lit everyone's faces like fire.

Luna squealed and pointed, and my heart remembered how to beat normally. I breathed deeply and tucked myself down between Mum and Aunt Izzy,

Luna's folded pram at my back. "I ran all the way to the playground," I said.

"Thank you so much," said Aunt Izzy, leaning her head briefly against my shoulder.

Luna grunted and pulled at her mother's arms, reaching for me.

I smiled as green and blue fireworks flashed high in the sky and accepted her happily. I wouldn't have asked to hold her, of course; Aunt Izzy must have been frantic, and if I'd been her I'd have never wanted to let precious Luna go again. But I was relieved for the chance to hold her all the same. I squished her tight for a moment, straightened her little cream coat with the bunny ears on the hood, and set her in my lap.

The fireworks went for a full half hour, dazzling lights fountaining up from the barges on the lake, showers exploding in the sky, love hearts expanding out like the very universe itself high among the stars. Red, blue, green, gold; white and purple and pink. Glittering light after glittering light, the pulse and beat of the pop music medley they'd been set to pounding out from countless speakers around us as people listened on their phones, on bluetooth speakers, even on old-fashioned portable radios.

It felt strange not to move once they were over. For fifteen years I'd witnessed this autumn spectacle and afterward, there'd been the immediate flurry of bodies as everyone rose, hunting through the dark for misplaced belongings, folding mats and packing bags and heading en masse to their cars, scattered throughout the surrounding suburbs.

So now, the sixteenth time I'd seen them... The quiet afterward was strange.

Not unwelcome, though; it was quite pleasant to simply sit and absorb the night. Chatter was slow to restart, and although the hundreds-strong crowd murmured and muttered, there was something subdued about the quality of the sound compared to before the fireworks.

Luna snuggled down on my lap, her head leaning heavier and heavier against my left arm.

I shifted a little, trying to prop the weight against my thigh, and Aunt Izzy reached over to tuck a soft blue blanket over my lap, and over Luna.

I smiled a little as Luna battled her heavy eyes; they fluttered and flittered as she fought desperately to stay awake, but it was a losing battle, and within a few minutes, she was out.

I yawned.

In front of me, Harry glanced up from his phone. "Past your bedtime, princess?"

His teasing was goodnatured: it was a well-established fact in our family that Harry, even at the age of nine, was the night owl, and I was often the first person in the family to bed at night.

I was usually the first person awake too, of course. For me, dawn felt like a magical time of day, filled with fresh air and promises. I did my best work first thing in the morning as the light crept into the world, and I hated missing it; I felt agitated in some sort of inexplicable way when I hadn't seen the sun come up in the morning.

I stuck my tongue out at Harry. Of course I wasn't going to admit that curling up on the mat with Luna right now and joining in her nap sounded like a mighty fine idea.

I chatted with various family members for a while, and watched over Mum's head to my left as the moon grew higher and higher. Twenty minutes to go. Ten. Five.

"Should I wake her when it starts?" I asked Aunt Izzy. On the one hand, Luna was two and would remember about as much of this experience as I did of my first eclipse. On the other hand, it was kind of a special event.

"Wait until it really gets going," Aunt Izzy replied. "It'll take a while. She might as well get as much sleep as she can, she'll be a cranky beast tomorrow as it is."

I snugged Luna gently, careful not to wake her up. "Let me know if you want a hand," I said. I didn't have too much homework for once—I'd just handed a bunch of assignments in and it was still a few weeks until the end of term and the next round of tasks were due—and I didn't mind hanging out with Luna when she was cranky; I knew Aunt Izzy felt less guilty about letting Luna sit and watch TV for the afternoon if she was doing it with me, and I could binge watch the latest high school mega-drama at her house as easily as at mine.

"Thanks." Aunt Izzy patted my head fondly. "You're a good kid. Glad you belong to us."

I tilted my head into the patting.

A cry rang out in the crowd, and people began to point at the sky.

I pivoted toward the moon, and sure enough, a narrow sliver had been carved out along one edge. Something joyful buoyed in my chest, and I settled back on my hands, the pram propping me up, Luna curled on my crossed legs, Mum pressed against me on one side, and Aunt Izzy on the other.

Forty-five minutes later, as the eclipse was nearing totality, Luna stirred in my lap. I blinked sleepily. Watching the earth's shadow creep gradually over the moon had lulled me into a kind of liminal state, not asleep, but not really awake either.

Luna blinked to wakefulness too, making soft cooing sounds and managing a solid punch in my ribs as she stretched.

Then she saw the moon.

"Moon!" She sat bolt upright, both arms outstretched. "Moon! Luna moon!"

"Well," I said. "It's definitely the moon. I'm not sure it's yours though." I prodded her gently in her chubby cheek, grinning.

"Luna moon." She pouted, stretching harder and waving her hands, fingers flexing as she tried to grasp it.

"Sure, why not. Luna's moon."

Aunt Izzy, who had migrated to the other side of the mat to chat with another one of my aunty-and-uncle sets, glanced over. "Hey, bubba," she crooned.

Luna looked at her mother, then back at the moon, then back at her mother. "Luna want *moon*."

Aunt Izzy laughed in delight. "We named you right, didn't we kid. Well, I'm sorry, you can't have the moon, but you can have your bottle." She fished a sippy cup of milk out of one of the backpacks we'd brought in under the pram and waved it at Luna.

Luna clapped, rose in that delightfully unsteady way of all small people, and toddled toward her mother.

Partway there, she hesitated—"Moon!"—and turned to look at the moon again, now more than three quarters hidden by the shadow of the Earth.

I glanced up at the moon for a fraction of an instant—and frowned. A second ago, it had been mostly dark. Now, I could have sworn that the Earth's shadow was covering only half of it.

I blinked, furrowed my brows... What the heck?

I must have imagined things. The eclipse mustn't have progressed as far as I'd thought.

I looked back down.

Luna was gone.

"Luna?" Aunt Izzy stared at the place where a split second ago, her tiny daughter had been. "Luna!" Her scream cut through the sleepy aura that had settled over the crowd.

Around, people bolted upright as my parents and aunts and uncles and cousins fell over themselves to get to us, clamouring to know what had happened, where Luna was, where she'd gone, and how.

Aunt Izzy was beside herself, throwing herself to her feet and staring wildly around.

I jumped up to help—and a strange, piercing whistle cut through the noise.

I whirled around toward the food vendor's caravans upslope from us—and there, maybe forty metres or so away at the treeline behind the caravans, was the boy.

I shouldn't have been able to see his gaze from here, not in this lighting with the moon nearly gone. But I could. And he was staring right at us. At me.

Luna had vanished, and a strange boy who'd appeared now for the third time tonight was staring right at me. He'd whistled for my attention, and now he was crooking his finger at me, beckoning me toward him.

Pulse racing, I detached myself from my family group and wove my way toward him, picking a path through the mats and blankets and limbs of the crowd.

Close up, the scent of the food vendors filled my awareness again, popcorn and fairy floss and hot frying oil. It soured my stomach, and I pressed my hands against my belly to steady it.

Luna was gone—again—and this time the chances of finding her seemed even slimmer, because where on earth had she gone to, and how in the world were we going to get her back?

How did someone vanish, just like that?

As I neared, the boy disappeared around the corner of the popcorn caravan. I followed, heart racing, adrenalin sizzling through my chest, stomach queasy and discomforted. "What?" I said, snappier than I would have if my favourite two-year-old hadn't suddenly gone missing.

"I thought you'd want to see this," he said over the hum of the food vendors' generators. He led me a few steps away, toward the little carpark, and pointed.

There, on the high wall that separated the carpark from the main road, stood a silhouette, a child, precariously balanced, arms uplifted toward the moon.

"Luna!" I shouted.

The boy grabbed me by the arm as I tried to launch into a run. "Shhh," he said. "Don't frighten her, she'll fall."

I hated him for it, for grabbing my bicep like that, for the way his fingers cut through my hoodie, and for holding me back—but he was right. And so, jaw twitching, I shook him free and hurried at a fast walk up the steep slope of the carpark's exit to where the wall met the rising ground level, and I stepped out onto the pale, foot-wide strip of concrete with him right behind me. "Luna," I crooned gently. "Luna, Rory's here."

She ignored me, arms still raised to the moon in front of us—and it was definitely three-quarters eclipsed now. I must have been hallucinating earlier, or had something in my eyes, or...

Something.

"Moon moon moon, Luna moon." Luna gabbled happily to herself, wriggling her fingers, waving at the huge white rock in the sky above us.

I crept closer. *Please don't fall, please don't fall.* I wasn't quite sure if I was talking to Luna, or to me: in the middle, where the carpark dipped down to meet the grass that ran down to the lake, the wall was over a storey tall.

"Luna," I tried again. "It's me. It's me, Rory. Come give me a hug, snuggleberry."

Luna pivoted toward me. "Moon!" she said, face lit with delight as she pointed, hazel eyes wide.

"Yes, I see it," I said, nodding solemnly. "Big moon." I glanced at it. "Well. Not so big right now, but the eclipse is pretty cool."

"Moon hiding," Luna said, nodding back.

I grinned. "Yes, the moon is hiding."

"Luna moon?"

"Yes," I said, inching closer. "Luna's moon is hiding." I reached out, closer, closer… There. My hand closed around her shoulders. I drew her to me and held on for dear life, picking her up, sitting her on one hip, and more carefully than I'd done anything in my life, inching my way back to safety.

When I finally hopped off the wall to the grass, I remembered how to breathe again.

I hugged Luna to me, my cheek pressed against her baby-soft golden hair—and hoped desperately that she wouldn't disappear again.

The boy was staring at us intently. From this angle, in the moderate lighting of the carpark, he wasn't just cute—he was freaking *hot*. Dark hair just long enough to tussle, dark eyes intent and all-seeing, like he was looking right into my soul and found something there interesting.

I shook my head, and walked toward the carpark.

"Gale," he said, catching up with us—as though I was supposed to know what he meant.

"Sorry?"

"I'm Gale." He held out a hand, presumably for me to shake.

Unfortunately for him, I wrote fanfiction in all my spare time and I knew my tropes. I had four whole pages in my oh-so-important notebook that he'd teased me about devoted to reasons why mysterious strangers got involved in someone's life, and ninety percent of them weren't good.

I kept walking. "Cool," I said. "Thanks for finding her."

Not that he had, not quite, but whatever.

"I need to talk to you." His gaze hadn't let up, intense and scrutinising—and not just of me, but of Luna.

"Hold on," I said, shifting Luna to my other hip. I paused on the asphalt at the bottom of the carpark with the hum of the generators muffling the world and dug my phone out of my pocket. *I've got her,* I sent on the extended-family chat group, hoping that this would be another miraculous moment where the message would get through quickly.

It did. Within a second of sending the message, replies began flooding through—relieved and happy emoji, mostly, with a 'Phew' from Dad.

"Right," I said, tucking my phone away and scooching Luna up my hip a little. "Shoot."

He took a deep breath. "She's a meterogician." He nodded at Luna.

I blinked.

"Weather magic," he elaborated. "Well, mostly weather."

"Yeah, I figured that's what it meant," I said. "I just didn't realise you were serious."

He—Gale—shoved his hands deep in his pockets. "Look, you saw what she did with the moon just before."

"I didn't see anything." Why had my grip on Luna suddenly tightened? "She just likes the moon is all."

Gale sighed. "Aurora, you know that's not true."

My eyes widened. "How do you know my name?"

"Meteromagic is heritable," he said, ignoring my question as I pressed Luna tightly to me, arms wrapped firmly around her. "Runs in families. It's usually pretty low-level, though. Not like her." He nodded at Luna again.

"That's ridiculous," I said. "A, no such thing as magic. B, it's an eclipse and this is the twenty-first century, no one believes eclipses are magic any more. C, even if there *is* magic, even if the eclipse *is* part of it somehow, you said this magic is hereditary. No one else in our family is like that."

He arched an eyebrow at me pointedly in the stark white carpark streetlights.

"What?" I snapped. "*What*? Me?! Ah ha. Very funny."

He shrugged. "The name fits."

"Mate," I said acerbically, "I went to school with a kid named River. Didn't mean he could control the watershed." I arched my own eyebrow back at him. "Names are just names. You're being ridiculous. And creepy," I added, my brows furrowing. "Again: how do you know my name?"

"It's not just you two," Gale said, ignoring my question yet again. "Didn't you ever wonder where your uncle went?"

"No," I said, sassy, "because it's none of my business." I turned to leave.

A thought struck me and I whirled back to him. "Wait, have you been stalking me?"

"No!" he protested, hands flying up, palms out in a defensive position. "I was trying to get a second with you alone!"

"Alone? *Here?* Genius plan, stalker boy." I shook my head.

He folded his arms. "Not, like, alone-alone, just away from your billion and three family members for a second."

"Oh, right," I said. "That makes total sense, try to talk to me away from my family *at a family picnic.* Because it's *so* hard to pick a time when I'm *not* completely surrounded... by... them."

Oh. Okay. So he kind of had a point.

My cousin Neil was even in most of my classes at school.

Urgh.

But even so.

"Look," he said, rubbing at the back of his neck, "I know your name because I was sent to find you, okay? I have meteromagic too, and I was told to come find you and talk to you about it. You're Aurora, right? Dawn? I bet you're a massive early bird, think best first thing in the morning, that sort of thing? Only no one expected *her* to happen, the magic doesn't usually manifest until puberty, she's going to be hella strong, I can't even begin to imagine—"

"That's great," I cut in, breathing a little too fast of air that tasted like cold grass and, here in the carpark, the petrol used to keep the generators for the food vendors running. "But what the hell are you on?"

In response, Gale closed his eyes, head thrown back to the star-studded skies. Feck he was hot. "I'll show you," he said.

I could run. Or walk, at any rate. Walk away and go back to my family and pretend this never happened. I had a feeling, though, that Gale wouldn't be dissuaded as easily as that.

So I stayed—Luna was safe enough for now, happy in my arms as she watched the moon over my shoulder—and eyed him sceptically. "What, something dramatic is supposed to happen?"

"Shhh."

I snorted, but dutifully shhhed.

And shivered. Because out of clear night air, clouds were forming.

The chatter of the crowd began to rise over the humming of the generators—people frantically checking their weather apps, no doubt, because I didn't know about them, but our family had meticulously checked, rechecked, and re-rechecked the weather forecast tonight, and there had been nothing said about clouds of any sort, let alone...

Rain.

It was raining.

Fat, icy drops were landing on my head, my shoulders, the asphalt around me… and one splash-landed on my nose.

What the actual hell?

I stared up at the sky. A small, archetypal cumulonimbus had gathered right over the edge of the lake, spanning maybe a kilometre or so—and it was raining.

"No!" Luna pouted, and I knew from experience she'd be stomping her foot to go with it if she could reach the ground right now. "Moon."

"Yeah, kid," Gale said, eyes still closed, face tight like he was concentrating hard. "In a second."

"Moon."

The rain faltered.

"Moon!"

In an instant, the cloud burst outward and diminished, little wisps spiralling away into the night sky—and the moon, blood red and fully eclipsed, hung gleaming in the sky.

"Ouch!" Gale glared at Luna.

I stared at Luna.

"She did not just do that," I murmured.

There was a logical explanation for this. Of course there was. Sudden freak shower of rain, cloud freakishly disappearing…

That weird moment earlier where it looked like the eclipse had reversed…

Oh. Yeah. There was a logical explanation for all of this—and unfortunately, it looked like the one that Gale was offering.

"Well, crap," I said, studying Luna's adorable squishy face. "How are we going to convince her not to play around with this until she's older?"

"Come with me," Gale said at once. "There's an academy, they'll teach you, and her. They'll teach you everything, I'll teach you…"

I couldn't have raised my eyebrow any higher if I'd tried. "Or, here's an idea, I go back to my family, I tell them what I've learned, and we figure out how to manage it without the help of random stalker strangers."

"You can't tell them!" It was hard to tell in the white light, but it seemed like the colour drained from his face. "You can't tell them!"

"Or," I said, "I could." They were my family, after all, and hadn't he said this thing was supposed to run in families? Besides. There were practically thousands of us. Someone in the family was bound to have an idea that would help. There hadn't been anything yet we hadn't been able to solve.

"This is not usually this hard," Gale muttered, rubbing at his neck again.

"Excuse me, what?"

"Nothing."

"Did you just say, 'This is not usually this hard'? Not usually? Not *usually*? How many times have you done this, stalker boy?!" I leaned close, getting up in his space. "Five? Ten? Do you hang out at public gatherings every other night trying to wile girls away with your charms and your..." Well, I couldn't exactly call them lies, could I? Urgh. "Your, you know," I jiggled my chin in lieu of waving my hands, since they were full of Luna. "Stories."

"Three," he said, going a little red in the face. "I've done this three times before, for your information, and yes, usually the girls I talk to about this are grateful that I'm here to explain things."

"Usually," I said, "the girls you talk to are gullible." I whirled around and stomped away.

"Is that a no, then?"

I whirled back to him. "What, did I whisper? Of course it's a no!"

"You can't just tell people this!" he called after me. "They'll lock you up, you know. Take you to psychiatrists and have you examined and put you on all sorts of medication, and none of it will help! None of it will take the abilities away. It'll just mean that when the time comes, when they burst out of you without control, you'll have no idea what to do, and people will get hurt."

I cocked my head, eyes narrowed. "Thank you," I said, "for that lovely little insight in your life history."

He reddened further.

"But unlike exhibit A"—I nodded at him—"my family love me."

I left, and as I rounded the corner of the closest vendor's caravan, the salty, buttery smell of popcorn filled me with warmth physically as the realisation of what I'd said filled me with warmth emotionally.

I was right. My family did love me, exactly as I was, and I didn't need anything else. I wasn't a freak. I was… What was it Dad said? Not a freak, a unicorn.

I nodded firmly as I wove my way back through the crowd of picnic rugs and blankets, small children bedecked with glowsticks and large children playing tag, adults and children alike laughing and chatting and watching the sky.

I glanced up. The moon was huge, and round, and red.

"Moon!" Luna said gleefully. "Luna moon!"

"Yeah, kid," I said, pressing my cheek against her hair again. "It's Luna's moon."

Back at my mat, I deposited Luna into Aunt Izzy's grateful, desperate arms. I stared Aunt Izzy firmly in the eye. "Aunt Izzy," I said. "We need to talk."

As Time Whirls Slowly Past

ASHLEY GOT THE FRIGHT OF HER LIFE FOR THE THIRD time that day as she opened the laundry to be confronted by her daughter's Labrador-sized stuffed-and-wired unicorn—again. She sighed, pressed her hand to her chest, and waited for the adrenalin to subside.

Bloody hell. Maybe she just needed to wash it now and be done with it. She'd put it in here earlier this morning when her daughter Ellie had peed on it accidentally—'accidentally' was a common word in their house, these days—and if she was going to be super honest, she'd been avoiding cleaning it because it seemed all too hard. A lot of things seemed too hard right now. All she really wanted was a couple of days to herself—maybe a week if she was being greedy—just to rest, recoup, regather. To stop feeling stretched thin, like there were fifty-three too many things on her to-do list every day. To stop ending every night feeling like a failure.

But then, the kids had had vegetables for dinner—curry, no less—and they'd gotten through most of their school work for the day and no one had shouted or cried during witching hour.

Ashley had even managed to convince Ellie to go to sleep without the giant unicorn guarding her bed, a ten-out-of-ten success she'd never been able to pull off yet in the three years Ellie had owned the toy.

Adrenalin calmed, Ashley took a deep breath of laundry-power-scented air and ran a hand through her slightly itchy, slightly oily, dark hair. Man, a long shower would be nice, too. Uninterrupted, for preference, though with Carter up and down for an hour and a half every night these days, who knew how plausible that actually was.

She'd lock herself in the bathroom with her favourite blackberry bubble bar if she didn't know that he'd just sit outside the door and moan and whine until she got out and settled him again.

Ashley closed her eyes and let herself sag against the doorframe of the laundry, just for a moment. It wasn't defeat, it was regrouping. Just for a second.

And in five more days, Tom would be home. For good, with any luck, this time.

Five more days.

Ashley wound dirty clothes down into the washing machine, loaded it with powder and lavender fabric softener, listened to the music of the beeps as she adjusted the settings, and set the machine whirring.

She left the laundry with a sigh, snagged a glass of fresh-pressed orange juice from the fridge, and collapsed onto the couch in front of the TV.

Medical drama, white-guy movie, news, news, slapstick… Urgh. Netflix it was.

It was a little ritual she went through every night, and she wasn't even quite sure why, because there was never anything on free-to-air that she was interested in, and Netflix was *right there*, but she persisted with it nevertheless. She'd found, in the last twelve months of Tom being gone one week out of every fortnight, that it was the little, thoughtless rituals that kept you sane when everything else felt like it was falling apart.

Ashley picked out the latest period drama, set it playing, and picked up the embroidery she was working on.

Well, 'working on' was generous; she, like most of the rest of the world right now, was attempting to learn a few 'old school' skills while they were all stuck inside for months on end, and her first attempt at embroidering a row of flowers down the side of Ellie's little jeans looked more like a child's scribble—which was fitting, since Ellie's canvas of choice was herself whenever possible.

But this latest attempt, a little pair of flowering cacti in a pair of terracotta pots, was actually looking okay. Recognisable, anyway, and the colours made her happy.

Hopefully Ellie would like it.

Upstairs, footsteps creaked floorboards, muffled by worn carpet.

Ashley sighed. "What is it, Carter?"

Silence.

She set in a couple more stitches, working now on the pale pink stars that served for flowers on the cacti.

Creak. Creeeeak.

Ashley sighed again, but ignored the footsteps, focusing on the period drama where two lovers were melting each other with their gazes from across a room. She snorted. Who could have predicted that real life would have taken such a steep turn back toward eighteen-hundreds courtship.

Briefly, she imagined having to date in a situation like this, when you couldn't even visit someone's house, couldn't really go out in public, couldn't eat out or go to the movies or do anything typically date-ish.

Man. Dating was hard enough.

She blinked, shook her head, and refocused on her stitching. After ten years of marriage, that stage was *long* behind her. Thank God.

Creeeeak.

"Mummy..."

Her jaw twitched. "Yes, Carter?"

"I can't get to sleep."

"I know, sweetie. That's normal right now, remember?"

A protracted pause. She never quite knew if it was because he was processing what she'd said, or just that he was finally getting sleepy; he didn't tend to do it in the day time.

"Yeah."

The period drama's end-credit music trilled, overcut with a montage of scenes, shots of the main couple staring at each other across rooms, across gardens, staring longingly out of carriage windows at each other.

Ashley might not know what dating from a distance felt like, but she sure knew what marriage-at-a-distance did. She closed her eyes for a second, caught by momentary longing for her husband's arms around her. She tried to make herself believe that she could smell his aftershave, a little sharp, like mint, but soft like lotus and sandalwood too.

"Can I have a shower?"

That was Carter again.

Patience, Ashley reminded herself, *is a virtue*. "Yes, sweetheart. I'll come get you in a bit."

Upstairs, the sound of the hot water pipes screeched a little before settling into their steady, thrumming rhythm.

Chocolate would make everything better.

Ashley tucked her needle into the soft denim of

Ellie's jeans and set it all aside on the couch. In the kitchen, hidden behind the bright red toaster, was the kids' stash of Easter eggs. If she took a small one from each bucket, they couldn't complain about her being unfair…

She took a gold one from Carter's stash and a pink one from Ellie's, the foil slightly crinkled and gleaming brightly under the kitchen downlights. The foil went into the collection in the otherwise-empty fruit bowl—she'd heard somewhere recently that it could only be recycled in fist-sized balls, so they were clumping it all together as they collectively ate their way through the Easter harvest—and Ashley slumped back on the couch, tossing her feet up over the arm and twisting sideways, one arm lolloping over the side, fingers dragging on the cold tiles of the living room floor.

Which, by the by, was filthy, and she'd probably contaminated herself now with chocolate crumbs or toast crumbs or spilled milk or heck, even pee, who knew. The tiles were long overdue for a mop. Probably, she should do that before Tom got home. He'd appreciate it, she knew… But he also wouldn't judge her if she didn't do it.

The kids ate vegetables, she reminded herself. We walked around the pond twice. They only had two hours of iPad time today, a serious improvement on yesterday's seven hours apiece.

The shower shushed away overhead.

With another sigh—it seemed to be the only way she got any air, some evenings—Ashley hit pause on the TV, licked the last of the chocolate egg from the inside of her cheek, and headed upstairs to fish Carter out of the shower.

The bathroom was steamy and warm, a pleasant contrast to the cool evening downstairs. The smell of soap filled the air… and puddles covered the floor.

And the toilet.

And the carpet outside the bathroom, where child-sized wet footprints told the story of Carter going in to his sister's room to check on her before returning to his shower.

Ashley slumped, but grabbed a white towel from the linen press, wiped up the worst of the water, and rapped her knuckles on the shower's glass door.

Carter's broad, tanned face appeared through a hole he'd rubbed in the steam.

"Time to hop out," Ashley said, holding up the towel.

Carter's face disappeared, and the water shut off in the shower.

The door creaked open, and Ashley swaddled him in a towel big enough to wrap right around him twice. Seven years old, and he weighed barely any more than his four-year-old sister. Kid was all skin and bones—and muscle, she reminded herself as she towelled him down. He'd been doing gymnastics since he was five, the local club had scouted him at school, and he'd had a six-pack about that long to go with it.

She shook her head, lips pressed to hide a smile. "Love you, kiddo," she said as she finished drying him down and folded the towel neatly in half lengthwise.

Carter disappeared off to his bedroom to dress, and Ashley a moment to savour the warm, damp, soapy air, straightening the bath mat, hanging the towel, moving a stray bar of soap that had dried to the counter back to the soap holder over the bath.

"Mum." Carter reappeared in the doorway again, buttoning the shirt of his blue Transformers pyjamas. "Can I leave my light on?"

Valiantly, Ashley resisted the temptation to rub at her forehead. "Sure, kiddo." She couldn't keep the resignation out of her voice, though. "Why not."

She'd fought that one in the beginning, not wanting him to grow reliant on it. But she'd been terrified of the dark as a kid—she still remembered the time that the natural movement in her vision in the dark had seemed like a green, ugly witch's face taunting her from her bookshelves—and the alternative was either a prolonged fight, or her sitting up at the desk on the landing until he fell asleep.

Some nights, that wasn't a terrible proposition either; although the whole difficulty-with-bedtime thing drove her nuts, on another level she couldn't forget feeling exactly the same way when he'd been a toddler learning to settle himself at night as well, and how many hours she'd wasted lying on his floor teaching him to sleep—wasted because of her attitude, her frustration.

Those years had passed, and these would too, probably when the world finally went out of lockdown, whenever that might be.

In the meantime, it seemed prudent all round to avoid as many fights as possible.

She could train him out of using a light to fall asleep some other time, when the world *wasn't* falling apart around them.

"Mummy…"

Patience patience patience patience patience. "Yes, Carter?"

"I feel like there's something in my room."

Ashley couldn't help herself: she sighed again. "Hold on." She flicked off the heat lamp and the light bulb in the bathroom, went to close the door but changed her mind—keep it open, let it dry out—and crossed the tiny space that wasn't quite small enough to be a hallway but wasn't really big enough to be anything more than a landing for the stairs and went into Carter's room. "What's up?"

"I feel like there's something under my bed," he said, curled up in a ball, dwarfed in the queen-sized bed he'd inherited when Ashley and Tom had upgraded to a king. Carter peered up at her with big, brown eyes, pitiful and underscored by heavy dark circles.

"Kiddo," Ashley said, running her hand over his head, "you'd really feel a lot better if you could just go to sleep."

And she would feel better with her husband home, and time off from single-parenting, and enough energy to do everything she felt like she needed to do in a day to keep the household running.

Might as well point out how much better they'd all feel if Ellie's toy unicorn came to life and granted them all some wishes.

Momentarily distracted by the hypothetical question of whether or not unicorns could grant wishes, or whether that was something exclusive to genies or jinn, Ashley got down on her knees and peered under the bed.

Dust bunnies, more dust bunnies—a couple big enough to be dust hares—a slew of unpaired socks, a small stack of comic books, and a few pieces of Lego.

"There's nothing under there, Carter."

He nodded solemnly, but his expression didn't change.

Ashley thought longingly of her embroidery on the couch downstairs, her period drama, her hour and a half of alone time before she'd crash exhausted into bed.

The world wouldn't be like this forever.

And she wouldn't have the kids forever either.

With one last sigh, Ashley flicked off the light.

"What are you doing?" Carter squeaked in alarm.

"Move over," Ashley said. "I'll lie down with you for a bit."

A pause, that protracted silence again, though this time he was also moving over as he thought, making room for her amid the small horde of pillows and stuffed animals he hadn't particularly cared for until he'd acquired a baby sister who loved anything animal more than almost everything else in the world.

"Will you stay until I fall asleep?"

Dim light filtered in from the stairwell, and as she lay down, Ashley noted that Carter's blinds hadn't been drawn all the way down; a sliver of night sky showed, a few stars glimmering way out there beyond. Cold air diffused into the room from the crack, and for a moment she reached to close the blind...

But stars, like children, were something she never quite had the time to appreciate enough.

So she tucked Carter down in his blankets, pulled the uppermost one over her as well, draped her arm around the top of Carter's pillow so it rested against his fuzzy, warm head, and watched as the stars whirled slowly past beyond the silhouette of Carter's perfect, child-like face.

Across A Corpse-Like City

I'M HERE BECAUSE I HAVE TO BE, BECAUSE I HAVE TO record the last chapter of this story, because if I don't, then no one will. And if no one records it, then there'll be no record left of it anywhere on the planet, and I couldn't bear for all of this to have been in vain. It would be too much, too pointless—too painful.

Let's face it. It was probably in vain anyway.

Who's left to care whether I made it across town for one final journey or not?

…I care.

And if anyone comes looking—no, when *they* come looking, when it's finally been long enough that the contagion has cleared and the solar quarantines lifted… I want them to have a clear understanding of how this ended.

I want them to remember my name.

Is that selfish?

It's probably selfish. But when you're the only person left alive, maybe everything you do is, by default, a selfish act.

So I'm sitting here at the computer terminal at the port, the scent of the pine-based antiseptic still thick in the air— and it smells like futility, like lost hope.

This is what the end smells like: pine-based antiseptic and steel, stale air and musty carpet from the rain that leaked in through a broken window.

This is what is looks like: an empty terminal, commercial-grade navy-blue upholstery on the waiting area chairs, silver steel tech terminals sprouting in little clusters like so many mushrooms glinting in the light, sky-high ceilings containing nothing but echoing emptiness.

This is what the end sounds like: silence. Complete, utter silence.

Until the rain begins.

Fein stops writing for a moment, rests their head against the cool, sleek, silver of the terminal in front of them, eyes closed as pain squeezes their head in a vice. It's been happening more and more frequently, the vice-like headaches, with pain enough to spark little blue lights in the corners of their vision, sometimes enough to make them see ghosts and hear long-forgotten conversations. Enough to make them taste that bitter, dead-mouse taste on the back of their tongue.

They know this means the end is near, and that scares them, but it also comforts them as well, because at least then all this will be over, and they won't be alone anymore, because they'll either be nothing, or else they'll be something with all the rest of the people who have died.

It's the frustration that drove them here, weeks after everyone else gave up, days after the last of the power went out in the city, when the streets went black and silent.

It's hard to understand just how much noise electricity makes until it's gone.

Chills ran down Fein's neck the first time they stepped outside after that. They didn't live right in the centre of town, but they could see the scrapers from the crest of the hill by their house, the path they took to get powdered milk or freeze-dried cream from the store back in the early days of the disaster.

But that time, the last time, Fein paused under the spreading branches of a giant oak, its leaves gilded with fall and the late-evening sunshine both, and the scrapers on the horizon seemed more like monuments to greed, to stupidity, to hubris than they ever had to anything else.

Don't get them wrong, Fein's not anti-capitalist or anti-urban or any of that. Anti-greed, for sure, but that can be found anywhere that humans plague the universe. It's just that, that last time, with the sun glowing between the spires, the windows of the scrapers reflecting like so many diamond eyes, the city completely, utterly silent but for a single, paper-brown leaf scatterling down the asphalt of the road beside them, Fein knew that it was over, that everything had come to naught.

And so they'd begun the long, trudging road to the spaceport, way on the other side of the city, three days' travel in a world where cars no longer ran not because they or the roads were broken, but because of the contagion, the fact that people had been so totally and utterly cut off, and there was no one left to transport fuel.

The last petrol station had run dry two months ago. There'd been a riot. Two people had died.

It had barely made the news.

What were two more deaths against the millions—*billions*—that had already occurred?

And so now, all that was left was this: a three-day trek across a corpse of a city, smashed windows for empty eyes and skeletal, multi-story buildings like broken ribs jabbing the sky.

Fein lived alone, with a prolific and prosperous veggie garden out the back, a half-dozen chickens, and at the time of that epic journey across town, they hadn't left their house in eighty days.

Eighty-three, if you didn't count that one quick jog around the block for exercise, which sometimes they did count and sometimes they didn't.

They'd been out jogging, face flushed, body slick with sweat, ungainly bits that had grown more ungainly with the imposed confinement jiggling. Their heart had been pounding in their neck, they could taste sweat and thick saliva, and the sun had been slanting down through the red-turned leaves of the maple at the end of the street when they'd seen it: a woman, early-thirties, blonde, trim in her athletic wear in the way that broadcast long hours of bodily commitment—and pushing a black pram.

The woman had seemed fine. She was walking slowly, sure, but there was nothing about her that seemed to indicate what was about to happen—that she was about to drop dead, right there on the sideway, and the way her head bounced as it hit the ground still made Fein sick to the stomach.

Fein had rushed over, of course, despite the social distancing laws, risking tens of thousands of dollars in fines and maybe even imprisonment if they were caught by the wrong person. But they couldn't do nothing.

It was clear, though, that the woman was dead on impact: her neck lolled at an angle no live person would tolerate, her limbs splayed like an awkwardly crushed spider.

Fein couldn't quite bring themself to touch the woman—they'd been distancing for two years now, no one got close to a stranger without feeling awkward and uncomfortable—but they slipped their phone from the pocket, breathed on the screen once to see if it would fog, then held it in front of the woman's slightly parted mouth.

No fog.

No movement from her chest.

Struck by a brainwave, Fein opened the heart rate monitor app on the phone and held it so the woman's finger was against the sensor.

Nothing.

Carefully, holding it only by one corner, Fein tucked the phone back into their running vest's pocket, zipped it shut. With proper precautions, the phone could probably be decontaminated. The vest could go into the bin, wrapped in several layers of plastic to make them feel safe.

The pram bounced.

The baby, its occupant, cried out, a squirmy, uncomfortable sort of cry—and, horrified, Fein straightened and stared.

Dark-haired thing, chubby-cheeked. It was sitting and looking bright-eyed, so obviously not a newborn, but babies were as far outside the purvey of Fein's experience as flying, so who knew how old it might actually be.

"Hello? Baby?" Fein ventured.

The child lit up in a bright-eyed smile, gurgling and waving in that jerky, not-quite-controlled manner that babies did.

Well fuck.

Fein couldn't leave the baby here alone. Definitely couldn't take it home, either, not after its mother had just dropped dead.

Fuck fuck fuck.

Okay. Okay. They could do this. The woman would have a driver's licence, a wallet, something, and there'd be an address, and Fein could wheel the pram back and return the baby...

Hazmat. This called for hazmat protection first.

Ten minutes later—fastest suit-up they'd ever done—Fein was back on the scene, layered under three pairs of gloves and three pairs of leggings, everything tucked tightly first under their zip-up knee-length down jacket, then layered with a thin, ankle-length raincoat, topped with a blue plastic poncho for good luck. The top layer of gloves tucked over the sleeves of the raincoat; Fein wore not only a tightly-fitted surgical mask they'd been saving for an emergency but a balaclava and an impromptu helmet made from a white plastic shopping bag with a hole cut in it for their face, the ends tucked firmly into the neck of the raincoat under the poncho.

The baby was wailing. Either everyone else had chosen today to be sensible and stay indoors—like they were supposed to, like they'd been warned from the start—or else they'd heard the baby wailing and decided they wanted none of it.

Fein scowled, the mask rasping against their skin.

If they'd been sweating before, it was nothing to now: fall it might be, but the afternoons were still warm and long, and they were wearing approximately five billion too many layers for this. Already the sweat was dripping down their back, sticking uncomfortably under their arms, dampening their groin and wrists and neck.

Dizzy.

Damn.

Have to work fast.

Fein dug in the pockets of the woman's clothing fruitlessly, the cottony scent of the mask blocking everything else out, the baby's determined wails providing a soundtrack.

Ah, the pram.

There, in the bottom, a nappy bag. And there, in the nappy bag, a wallet. And there, in the wallet, a driver's license, and the baby only lived a street away, and thank heaven for that, because standing up too quickly sent a wave of dizzy nausea through Fein, and if they didn't get this over and done with, they'd pass out from heat stroke.

Quickly, confidently, as though they'd been doing it for years, Fein grabbed hold of the pram and pushed. They were surprised—having never actually pushed a pram before—by how easily the little vehicle moved; were all prams this smooth and effortless, or was this just a really expensive model?

One street up—the baby was now quiet again, staring sulkily at the surroundings, cheeks still red and blotchy from wailing—take a left, down the street with the strange yellow house and all the old rose bushes perfuming the air.

Number seven, there.

Fein wheeled the pram awkwardly up the single step into the red-brick house's front yard, closed in on the front door. Knocked. Was that their heart, hammering so loudly it sounded like someone else was knocking too?

Please be home. Please, someone, be home.

Because it was entirely plausible that no one was. Maybe this was a single-parent family. Maybe the other parent had been trapped elsewhere during the quarantine. Who knew? All Fein knew was that they *couldn't* leave the baby here on the doorstep, alone and unprotected, no matter what the prudent thing to do in terms of their own survival was.

Fuck. Was the baby still drinking milk? Was it eating food yet? The whole thing seemed more utterly overwhelming than the contagion itself, and that was saying much.

The door creaked open.

Thank God thank God thank you God.

"Is this your child?" Fein said, voice muffled by the mask.

"Alice!" the brunette-woman cried, flinging the screen door open compulsively before jerking to a stop, arms still outstretched toward the baby. "Where's Odette?"

The mother—other mother?—presumably.

Fein sucked in a deep breath, made a little harder by the mask that pressed against their face with the negative air pressure. "Dead."

They could have softened the blow, couched it in gentler terms… But the rigidity that came over the brunette woman in the doorway, the fear, the horror in her eyes… Best to rip the bandaid off quickly.

The brunette woman's jaw twitched. Her fingers clenched. "Oh," she said simply, then reached out to take the pram, bundling it inside, scooping out the child and hugging it close.

She knew. Fein could tell she knew.

But there was nothing else to say, no help or hope to offer, and so Fein walked away, wondering how long the two other members of Odette's household would be able to fight off the contagion that had breached their home.

That was the last human contact Fein had.

Eighty-three days ago.

And now they were dead, all dead, and as Fein walked along the deserted street, scrapers lining the forward horizon with the setting sun behind them, red-brick houses with white trim cloned in long rows down the sides of the road, abandoned vehicles in driveways and on road sides, tears clogged at Fein's nose, throat, thoughts.

They were the only one left.

It was *possible* that somewhere in the city, others still sheltered singling like they did. Possible. But the streets had been dead silent—pun fully intended, because a little black humour was the only way to stay sane when you were possibly the only person left on the planet—for at least a month now, and the radio broadcasts and tv stations had fallen silent three weeks ago, and Fein could feel it in the air that suddenly tasted clean, like a giant rainstorm had been through—or like they were out in the middle of a forest, like they'd used to do as a kid, hiking far away from human civilisation.

And everything was silent, and the power had finally gone out, and the nights were getting cold…

And this morning, the second day of the hike across town, Fein had woken up with a headache.

That was the problem with the contagion. Normally, deadly plagues burned themselves out; they killed their host far too quickly, incapacitating them before they could spread the disease to many other people.

Colds and flus and things like that were much worse, because you were contagious for days before you felt symptoms, and even when you *were* symptomatic, there was pressure to just keep going about your daily life anyway, maybe with a day or two off if you got *really* sick.

But this contagion had managed to marry the best with the best—or the worst with the worst, if you were human and not the virus.

It had taken fully eight months of research to realise that people could carry the virus for the better part of a month before they showed any symptoms—if they ever showed symptoms—and in that time, could have infected almost everyone they met.

The exact mechanism of transmission was still unconfirmed, but the assumption was that it passed in bodily fluids like most other viruses—sneezes, coughs, those sorts of things—and, unlike most other viruses, could live for several weeks outside a host body.

That was the death knell right there: a month-long, asymptomatic incubation period, the ability for the virus to last for weeks outside a host...

Fein shook their head. They could have told everyone that the shutdown came too late, that the world should have been more cautious the minute random flare-ups started appearing without any visible cause, or link to prior cases.

But the hospitals were already overloaded by that point, people dying in the hallways from lack of beds, lack of staff, and it was all just disaster processing, constant triage, and despite the apparently-united, superficially-logical approach of the world leaders, underneath it all, they were panicked too.

Fein's jaw twitched. Mistakes were made. Fatal mistakes. And the lives of the many were dictated by the decisions of the few.

And now they had a headache, even though they'd been sleeping outside in the cold, not wanting to risk entering anyone's house for anything, in case the contagion lingered, even though they hadn't seen another living soul for nearly three months.

But Fein had blinked to wakefulness under the oleander bush they'd spend the night in, blinking rapidly in the dim morning light, lungs full of the scent of dirt and grass and sappy leaves, the taste of bitter greenness in the back of their throat, and Fein had stared through the leaves at the overcast sky and realised that the shivers they were feeling weren't all from being cold, and the pain behind their eyes probably wasn't thirst.

It was the end, or the beginning of it, at any rate.

They still wanted to get to the spaceport, though. Make one final broadcast and see if anyone responded. Call out to the city and see if anyone was still alive, call out to space and see if the others had changed their mind and would come to the rescue after all.

If nothing else, to record their final days somewhere others might find it, decades hence when the far-flung reaches of humanity came toddling back to see what had happened to good old Earth after all.

And so, despite the headache, and the bitter green taste, and the inclement weather, Fein got up, and continued walking through the graveyard that had once been called a city.

Now, with Fein slumping at the terminal in the spaceport, the rain gushes down from the sky, a fall torrent here to cleanse the world. Fein hopes the animals will enjoy their new world; in fact, they know the animals will, because already in the last twelve months the reports from various science groups and environmentalists were indicating a far more rapid recovery on nature's part than anyone could have expected. Turns out, it wasn't humanity the planet was allergic to, just the frenetic pace. Given the chance to stop, to slow down, to breathe a bit, the planet was suddenly doing quite fine.

That tears at Fein's chest a bit, because it would have been nice to stick around, to watch as the Earth recovered and maybe make a go at real balance, find a way for humans to live in harmony with their environment for a change—and with themselves, their own bodies and psychological needs.

That would have been fun.

But the headache is stabbing like a knife now, the worst yet, and Fein knows that's one of the final signs. Likely it was a headache like this that scythed through the woman's head as she dropped dead on the pavement, inadvertently abandoning her child.

Lucky Fein, at least, has no one left to abandon.

They rest their head against the cool of the terminal—because what does skin contact matter now?—and watch as the rain thunders down beyond the distant plate-glass windows. The sun is dying on the horizon, a mere sliver of golden light that makes the grass oddly luminous, a vibrant, emerald green under the grey-blue clouds.

The roar of the rain on the roof is like the sound of one of the ships taking off, though without that deep, chest-gripping bass.

It's soothing.

They are, they think, quite happy to die here, like this.

Well, happy may be an overstatement, Fein isn't *happy* to die, no one has been, not in this context, not in these days, but if death has to come, then let it be like this, in the vast, cavernous waiting hall where people come to transit from one world to another, with the life-giving rain pelting down.

The terminal beeps, a green incoming-message light flashing on its periphery.

Fein bolts upright.

That isn't supposed to happen.

These terminals are public, they aren't made to call in on. Sure, someone talented with IP addresses and suchlike could probably hack one, ring in... But who in the world is left to do that?

Fingers trembling, breath catching like the agony of hope in their throat, Fein reaches out and answers the in-coming call.

Because of course, the answer is obvious.

Obvious, and plausible… But utterly, completely improbable.

"He… Hello?" Fein spoke too soon, the connection's still going, forging a bridge between Fein at their terminal here, and someone, somewhere, out there, *alive*.

It doesn't usually take this long to connect.

Fein's heart contracts again, a little squeeze of adrenalin, and they frown it away, impatient, because hope has let them down oh-so-many times before.

But with one last flash of black, the image on the screen resolves, and it's grainy, and it's black-and-white, and it's staticky and stuttery and Fein begins to cry, because it's beyond anything they could have hoped for, because it's Admiral Marchalle herself, commander of the legendary, semi-mythical space fleet, born from the one generational ship that set off for Alpha Centauri a century ago, and she's here, and she's talking to Fein, and Fein had better stop gawking and listen, because this, this very moment right here, will change the course of the human race forever.

"I'm sorry," Fein says loudly, leaning in to the terminal instinctively. "I'm having trouble hearing you."

"Situation. Report," Admiral Marchalle says crisply, also leaning forward a little, her beret pinned at its neat angle and her eyes flinty and tense even through the poor picture quality.

"All dead," Fein says, because this was the last city in the country left standing, and for all Fein knows, they are probably the last person left alive on Earth.

"Right." Admiral Marchalle nods, everything she does crisp and precise. "Standby for pickup in twelve hours."

"I… might not last that long," Fein replies as pain stabs through their head again.

Marchalle frowns. "Hang on." She speaks rapidly to someone off screen, nods, then turns back to the camera. "We're teleporting you down a shot of the vaccine. You'll have to administer it yourself, we can't get someone down to you fast enough, but it's a simple enough procedure and an intramuscular injection will do just fine."

Fein is dreaming. That's the only rational explanation.

The headaches are so intense they're causing hallucinations, and Fein is imagining the one thing humanity has hoped for more than anything else: that the space-humans, with their radically evolved technology, born from the discovery on Alpha Centauri of an ancient civilisation, would come through for dear old Earth, would have a magical solution that Earth, with all its billions and billions of clever, creative, wonderful humans, could never manage.

"Hello? Hello, can you hear me?"

"Y… Yes, I can hear you. Where will I find… the vaccine?"

It's so wildly implausible. Teleportation? Fein had known that the spacer-humans had advanced—but apparently even the Earth's wildest conspiracy theories had been underprepared for just how far that advancement had gone.

"We'll send it right to you," Admiral Marchalle responds. "Hold tight."

Sure enough, a perspex case appears on the dirty laminated floor next to Fein.

Hardly daring to breathe, they pick it up, unclick the latch, flip the lid open…

The needle is long, and thick, and this is going to hurt. But it's not going to hurt as much as dying, so Fein picks up the syringe, holds it upright like they've seen in the movies, and taps to remove the air bubbles. "Like this?" they say.

Marchalle nods. "It's hard to get wrong. Just stab it into your thigh, squeeze slowly until all the liquid's in, and remove the needle. Hurts like a bitch, but what choice do you have?"

Fein nods, swallows, tenses. Marchalle's right, and it's going to hurt like a bitch, and the rain is thundering down on the roof like it's determined to purge the world, and this is the end…

"Is there anyone else?" Fein asks, gaze flickering back to the screen.

Marchalle's mouth goes tight. "A few," she says. "One on your west coast, a couple in central Australia, three from Africa. There's a Pacific island that made it."

It's so many more than Fein could dared have hoped for… and it's few, so, so precious few.

The rain thunders down, the scent of pine-cleaner fills the air, and it's the end of the Earth at least for now, because how can so few people rebuild?

But Fein stabs the needle into their leg right as another wave of headache grips their head, grits their teeth, pushes the plunger slowly, slowly—Marchalle was right, it hurts like a bitch—and removes the needle, panting, and it's also a beginning, and that's far, far more than Fein could have dared to hope for.

"Well done," Marchalle says with a strained smile. "We'll see you in twelve hours."

The terminal goes blank.

Stiffly, dazed, head pounding and thigh aching, Fein lies down on the hard, cold floor. And, lullabied by the rain, Fein sleeps deeply for the very first time in months.

More Than Mushrooms

THE SILENCE WAS NOT GOLDEN, BECAUSE THE BREEZE was just a little too fresh for that, but it was definitely silver, or some other kind of precious metal. It was the kind of silence you only got out of doors, away from the buzz and hum of city electricity, away from *humanity*.

Lily, as an extrovert and an optimist, generally approved of humanity. But she defied even the most optimistic extrovert to remain entirely upbeat after three straight weeks housebound with two small kids and a restless husband, whose introverted nature was taking a pounding.

Hence: the silver silence of the outdoors.

Here, in this secluded gully full of knee-high bracken fern, bordered by radiata pines in drunken, staggering rows, the wind was the only thing Lily could hear right now, and as cliched as it felt to call it that, it was utterly refreshing.

Somewhere down below, at the bottom of the gentle slope a hundred or so metres away, were her husband and the kids. They hadn't gone far, just beyond sight, with but the pine branches hiding them and the wind sweeping their chatter away from her, Lily might just as well be alone.

She smiled. Leaned back on her wrists, adjusting one as it slipped a little on the emerald sleeping bag they'd brought from the car as a makeshift picnic rug, the actual picnic rug that lived there having gone temporarily and mysteriously missing.

In front of her, a little cloud of midges investigated the mostly empty plastic picnic cups, the last dregs of pink milk in the bottom of them apparently intriguing the little insects. The taste of the milk still hung at the edges of her mouth, sweet and sugary like decadence and family intimacy.

The breeze changed directions for a moment, and Lily wrinkled her nose at a familiar smell: she'd spent quite a bit of time hiking around in pine plantations, and every so often this smell, the one that smelled like the kids had left the toilet unflushed after a particularly intense episode of use, reared its head.

It wasn't quite like poo, she allowed, turning it over in her mind as she inhaled. How would she describe it? Poo-*ish*. A little more like dirt. Like decay. Perhaps a touch mildewy or mushroomy.

The mushroom bit might make sense. Half the reason they were here, after all, was that her husband had gotten it into his head that he wanted to try mushroom hunting, come after the saffron milk caps that had an apparent affinity with pine forests the world over. They were easily identified, moderately easy to find, and reportedly quite tasty, according to a bunch of local YouTubers. Benjamin, their eight-year-old, had supported the idea with unbridled enthusiasm. And both the kids needed a run, and Lily was happy to get out in the fresh air, and so after double-checking the permissibility of their actions, here they were.

Thank goodness the national parks were still open in their area.

Lily breathed deeply again, feeling the tension drain away from her shoulders, her chest.

There hadn't been any mushrooms here at the top of the gully, and maybe her family would have more luck down in the bottom where they'd gone exploring, but even if they returned home empty handed, not a one of them would return home empty-souled. And at this point, that was all Lily could ask of the world: all she wanted was for the kids to get through this with a minimum of trauma, for them to be happy.

Another deep breath—the air fresh and clean again now, the wind having swung back around—and Lily smiled. A tiny slice of heaven, that's what this was.

Her gaze lit on something across the other side of the gentle gully, maybe ten, fifteen metres away just in the border of the pines. The rusty needles were lifted and scuffed in places, as though perhaps a new crop of mushrooms were rearing their heads under-neath—they'd check, but the only ones they'd found in that area so far were slippery jacks, with their spongey yellow undersides, and her husband was a little suspicious of eating those even though they were, notionally, edible—and just there, a couple of trees back in a hollow between the dry, needleless lower branches, was something vibrantly green.

Lily stared, curious but too languorous to get up and investigate. Too bright for anything natural, it was a limey sort of green, and shiny. Probably litter, from prior mushroom hunters. Her husband had said after his preliminary investigation that it did look like others had been here recently.

Litter made sense.

A shout from the bottom of the gully drew Lily's attention; it was Benjamin, reappearing in his black shirt and camo pants that he'd picked out especially for their 'adventure'. She had no idea what had piqued his attention—not that it took much for him to raise his voice, they were constantly reminding him that 'inside voices' were a Thing—but his body language was animated and joyful, and it brought a smile to Lily's face.

His dark hair was getting long; they'd have to break out the clippers tonight.

His sister appeared through the pines behind him, entirely inappropriately dressed in unicorn jeans and a too-thin shirt for the weather, her hand tightly clasped in her father's. She was chatting animatedly too as Russell swung her up and over a blackberry bramble, nearly bare-caned as winter approached.

With a sigh that weighed more of contentment than resignation, Lily scrambled to her feet and began repacking their makeshift picnic away in the reusable orange shopping bag that had served as a basket. She rolled the chips packet down with a crinkle, tucked them into the bag and licked her fingers, stealing the last skerrick of salty, vinegary flavour. The last cheese roll, the rest of the pink milk, the half box of end-of-season plums that had been on sale in the corner store… Lily gathered it all back into the bag and straightened, hands on her lower back as she leaned side to side and stretched.

That lime green thing in the fringe of the pines still bothered her. There really was no excuse for littering except laziness, and she'd been trained early and often about the magnitude of that particular sin. One didn't live in debt to others if one could at all avoid it.

With a little sniff outward through her nose, Lily left the shopping bag with the sleeping bag-turned-picnic mat and picked her way through the sporadic brambles and bracken fern across the head of the gully.

She smiled wryly as she passed a slippery jack her son had kicked over, exposing its spongy yellow underside to the sun. It didn't especially bother her if they found no edible mushrooms today. On the one hand, she was pretty confident that the saffron milk caps were hard to misidentify. On the other... Well, it was eating wild mushrooms.

Under the fringes of the trees, where a frond of needles prickled at her forehead and the wind felt cool, the lime green thing sparkled on the ground, nestled by a stray tussock of vibrant grass and half covered by a little hump of rust-coloured needles. Lily bent, frowning. She'd thought at first it might have been a chip packet or some such, that shiny, metallic-looking material that was actually just disguised plastic.

But no. It *looked* like a chip packet or similar, but it was completely blank, no branding, no labels, nothing. And it looked thicker than the metallic plastic stuff they used for chips, a synthetic leather or something perhaps.

She picked it up, surprised at the weight of the little pouch, about the size of one of those little individual serves of chips. Definitely some sort of fake leather-like fabric, with something sort of knobbly inside. But darn if she could open the thing—there didn't seem to be any trace of a zipper or press studs or anything as she turned it over in her hands. Only a neat and definite row of thick stitching across one end—professional, though, like it had been made that way, not like someone had done it at home with a needle or machine.

Behind her, halfway down the gully, the children shrieked with laughter.

Lily whipped around toward them, blinking. For a second, she'd forgotten she wasn't alone. Frown weighing down her lips, knotting her eyebrows, she paced back out of the trees again and waited while Russell hiked the last of the way through the brambles and ferns with little Angel swinging in his arms.

It had grown darker, and Lily glanced up at the inclement clouds. A good moment to make their exit.

Sure enough, as Russell approached, fitful rain began to spit from the sky, teeny tiny droplets that bore an icy prickle that belied their size.

"What have you got there?" Russell asked as he drew near. He popped Angel down on the ground—she giggled—"Again, Daddy! Again!"—and came to Lily.

He smelled of clean sweat and pine, and instinctively Lily took half a step closer so they stood shoulder-to-shoulder. "I don't know," Lily said. "A pouch or something. I found it just over there in the trees. It doesn't seem to open."

Wordlessly, Russell accepted it from her and turned it over and over, squeezing it gently and holding it up to his ear to hear the gentle clinkish sort of sound. He shrugged, handed it back. "No clue," he said. "Someone must have left it here."

Lily rolled her eyes. "Well *obviously*, I highly doubt it grew here."

Russell grinned.

"What do I do with it?"

Russell shrugged again. "No clue," he said, and turned away to snag Benjamin as he went pelting past. "Hey, kiddo, grab the sleeping bag will you, it's time to go."

"Awwww." Benjamin pouted, but picked up the sleeping bag regardless, bunching it up in his arms with a rustling sound almost like feathers. Rain splattered it erratically, little dark spots on the deep green of the synthetic fabric.

"I'll take it with us," Lily said, tucking the strange green pouch into their orange shopping bag anyway. "Even if it's rubbish, it should go in a bin."

Russell smiled fondly at her over Angel's dark hair; he'd picked her up again and was holding her parallel with the ground over his shoulder as she shrieked with delight. "Sure," he said. "Whatever makes you happy."

Lily shook her head, half exasperated as ever at her husband's lackadaisical approach to litter, and half in love, as ever, with his willingness to do whatever did make her happy.

They bundled their way up the remainder of the slope to where they'd left the car on the side of the orange-dirt road, packed in their things and then the children, and head back for town.

At home that night, after the children were in bed and Lily and Russell were tucked up on the leather couch under a couple of blankets watching TV, Lily tipped her head back against the lounge and closed her eyes. "I think I'll put a message up on Facebook or something," she said.

She wriggled her toes under the blankets, pleased at how quickly they'd warmed up; the air tonight was chill, but it was too early in the season to turn the heaters on yet—they took a day or two to really start kicking in and warming the house, so there was never any point just turning them on for an evening.

The aroma of wild mushrooms perfumed the air, meaty and savoury and somehow just a little more delicate and complex than store-bought portobellos—they'd spotted some of the milk caps on the side of the road after all, as they'd been leaving the forest, and after the kids had gone to sleep Russell had fried them up with butter and tried them on toast, a willing canary testing the safety of their find. His verdict had been positive, and Lily had to admit that they'd smelled pretty amazing.

Maybe they'd try again in another couple of days; the rain had settled in as they'd driven home, and that was supposed to be good for bringing a new crop of mushrooms up.

The TV droned on, some YouTube channel Russell was into at the moment about remaking old cars and such.

"Hmm?" Russell murmured idly, tilting his head toward Lily.

"The pouch thingy," she said, nodding toward the kitchen where her shiny, lime-green find still sat in the makeshift picnic bag. "I don't know. I've never seen anything like it, I'm not sure what it is, and I just feel like someone is going to be missing it."

"Sure, honey," Russell agreed. "Stick it up in the local BSS group or something."

Lily nodded firmly and reached out to snag her laptop off the nearby coffee table.

It was a matter of minutes to open her browser, find a local Buy-Swap-Sell group on Facebook that seemed promising, and post a message about the object she'd found. She didn't add a photo; she deliberated over that decision, but in the end a photo was more likely to attract collectors who wanted to claim… whatever it was, simply because it was there, and it was unusual.

Smallish green pouch, reasonably heavy, found in pine plantation out past Urriara. PM for more details.

If the real owner was looking for it, they'd know what she meant.

It would have to do.

As Lily sat at her desk with her over-sized head-phones on and a mint-scented candle burning near-by, the sharp 'ding' of a notification on her laptop sent her scrambling for the mute button, both on the laptop itself and on the zoom meeting she was currently 'participating' in.

Reading articles about local mushrooms while listening to the call was participating, right?

And anyway, her team leader was only telling them exactly the same information the boss had emailed two days prior, it was nothing new—confirmed: out of the office for the next four weeks, office phones diverted so they'd send voicemails as email, make sure you don't contact clients out of hours, ensure that you take time to exercise regularly and sign off on your work health and safety paperwork before next Tuesday, et cetera, et cetera, blah blah.

Honestly, Lily was so sick of zoom she'd stab herself in the eyeball if she thought it would do any good, but the bosses were treating it like it was the best Christmas gift they'd ever had, so here she was. But if she was going to be stuck on calls that did nothing more than repeat information she already had, darn it all if she wasn't going to make good, multitasking use of the time.

And so, mushroom research it was. It was at least as productive as listening to Alfred whine about how his desk chair at home didn't lower to the correct height.

The kids had gone to sleep like a dream last night after spending a few hours running around in the bush, so as soon as the rain let up again, they'd go back and roam around some more, look for some more mushrooms, that sort of thing.

Assuming she didn't get fired, of course, for her bloody computer dinging notifications at her on a business call.

Mind you, Sally's cat had plonked itself on top of Sally's keyboard last week, right as she was supposed to be demonstrating a fiddly new procedure to the rest of the team, and she hadn't even been reprimanded, so perhaps a computer ding was just par for course these days.

Still, Lily scrolled through her open tabs as Alfred blathered on, trying to find the source of the interruption so she could avoid future embarrassment.

Ah, Facebook.

That was why she hadn't recognised it.

Trying to look like she was utterly intent on Alfred's chair issues, Lily opened her messages and found the source of the notification: someone had messaged her about the bizarre green pouch.

A Margaret A, who, judging by her profile picture, was maybe in her fifties and probably loved cats, and had two probable-grandchildren who looked to be about the same age as Lily's kids.

Hello, Lily. Is the green pouch you found shiny sort of chartreuse, soft leather, about 15cm long?

For no discernible reason, Lily's pulse sped up.

Yes.

Three dots popped up, bobbing up and down as Margaret A typed out a response.

And you found it in the Blue Rocks Waterhole Plantation, near the corner of East-West Rd and Blue Rocks Rd?

...That seemed plausible? Lily bit her lip, then, fighting the urge to bring up a map and double check, typed, *Yes.*

Is the pouch still sealed?

Lily felt like she was getting repetitive, but nevertheless, *Yes,* she typed—then added, *It is,* just for some variation. Was it still sealed? Heck if she knew how to open the thing.

Ah, lovely, Margaret replied, almost immediately. Fast typer, if nothing else. *What is your address, and when is it convenient for me to collect it?*

Lily nearly smiled, then remembered she was faking interest in the work call. *Working from home these days - aren't we all? - so any time is fine.*

She added her address—and realised Alfred had stopped complaining about his chair and their team leader Scott was wrapping up the meeting.

Quickly, Lily flicked back over to the zoom window, nodding sagely as though Scott's final comments were the most important thing she'd heard in her life, and managed to wave a convincing goodbye in approximate synchronisation with everyone else before leaving the meeting.

Phew.

She sat back in her chair and stared for a moment at the flickering flame of the minty candle, inhaling one of her favourite scents deeply and tilting her head sharply to one side. Her neck cracked satisfyingly.

Right.

Facebook. Margaret A.

Lily swiped back to her browser again and saw Margaret's latest message: *Is 5pm tonight convenient?*

The wording made Lily smile a little. *Yeah,* she replied. *5pm is fine.*

By the time 5pm rolled around, the rain had well and truly set in. It put a bit of a damper on any prospect of walking the kids around the pond, but they'd survive being locked up for a day. Thank goodness they'd had a big run yesterday.

They were now busily ensconced in front of the TV, playing a virtual gardening game on the Xbox that kept them entertained and at least was mostly free of violence.

The shower in the ensuite hissed as Russell transitioned from work mode to home mode, and Lily bustled around the kitchen, loading the dishwasher and cleaning off the bench in preparation for making dinner. She wrinkled her nose at the smell in the sink—Benjamin had tipped cereal in there and a bunch of it had caught in the plug that sieved out garbage before it could run down the drain. Gross.

She twisted out the plug, shook it a few times to stop it dripping so much, then carried it in her cupped hand to the bin.

Someone knocked at the door.

Lily stared at the goop in her hands for a second, gave her head a little shake, and tapped the gross cereal remains into the rubbish. "Coming!" she shouted. Quickly, she dropped the plug back into the sink and rinsed her hands.

Drying them on a dishtowel that had been lying over the fruit bowl, Lily sniffed. At least the kitchen smelled better now, the scent of lemon cleaner overpowering most everything else.

At the front door, a woman with reddish-brown hair and careful, neat makeup stood a few paces away, hands clasped in front of her. Her baby-blue blouse was neatly pressed, her slacks crisp—although damp spatters around the cuffs proved she had, at least, walked to the front door instead of levitating, as her otherwise perfect appearance suggested.

"Hi," Lily said brightly as she opened the screen. "You must be Margaret."

Ah, there was an umbrella, a slightly-whimsical clear plastic one, neatly folded behind the potted azalea, which was just starting to bear tightly-furled white buds.

The woman nodded. "You must be Lily."

Lily smiled as the aroma of rain-soaked earth curled around her. "Ordinarily I'd ask you in. But these days…"

Margaret smiled in response, warmth crinkling her dark eyes. "Of course. I'm happy to wait here." She lifted a hand a little, gesturing at the roof covering the entryway.

"Just a sec." Lily ducked back down the hall and in to the master bedroom. The bed was a mess, the covers twisted and folded over themselves—Russell had reverted to his natural sleep patterns, i.e. 1am to 10am, and rarely remembered to straighten the bed out when he got up, not that Lily minded—and the lime-green pouch sat on Lily's bedside table, perched somewhat precariously on a stack of crisp, new paperbacks.

Russell's cucumber-scented shower gel wafted out from the en suite on the warm, damp air of the shower. Snatching up the pouch, Lily closed her eyes briefly to enjoy the warm air, then headed back to the front door.

"This is your pouch?" she said, holding it up to show Margaret as she opened the screen door again. Goosebumps rose on her arms; the air out here was markedly cooler than in the bedroom.

Margaret's whole appearance was one of control and collectedness, but even so the relief in her eyes was palpable as she reached for the pouch. "Yes," she said. "That's it."

The way she took it, cradling it in both hands as though it was, perhaps, a small baby, caused Lily to tilt her head. "Do you mind if I ask how you lost it?"

Margaret made brief, nearly furtive, eye contact. "You didn't open it, did you." Statement, not question.

"No," Lily said with a small, wry smile.

Margaret sighed deeply, pressed the pouch to her chest, then picked at the seam across the top with long, natural-pink nails—and voila, the thick threads of the seam unravelled, reminding Lily of the bulk cloth bags of rice you could buy from the supermarket that came with a zipper but were initially stitched closed, presumably to prevent accidental rice spillages in said supermarkets. The tucked-in ends of the pouch that had been sewn shut opened out, and then Margaret tipped up the pouch, spilling the contents into one cupped hand.

Small, bluish-grey rocks, rough and raw but with a gorgeous intensity to their colour.

Lily's eyebrows shot up.

"It was stupid of me," Margaret said, and abruptly Lily realised just how much of Margaret's mannerisms and appearance were at odds with what she'd expected of someone who'd lost a pouch in a remote pine forest where mushrooms were found. "But my grandchildren—my granddaughter, it was her birthday on Tuesday, and of course we couldn't have a party with the pandemic going on, so we decided to head out to the forest. She'd just been reading *Small Mice, Big Mushrooms*, you know that new children's book?"

Lily nodded; she did, in fact, know the book Margaret was referring to, because Benjamin had been watching readings of it obsessively on YouTube last week and that's half the reason Russell had got it into his head to take the family mushroom hunting in the first place.

She grinned. "I bet your granddaughter couldn't wait to go mushroom hunting after that."

Margaret's eyebrows rose mildly. "Your children too?"

Lily nodded and leaned against the doorframe, shifting her weight onto her left leg and crossing her right one over. "And my husband."

Margaret grinned at that one, an infectious expression that lit up her eyes and made her seem much younger. "This," she said, lifting the hand full of rocks, "was supposed to be my birthday present to her. I was going to hide them under a tree or two and let the kids go fossicking. But by the time we carried all the things down out of the car, the pouch had fallen out, and we couldn't find it anywhere." She shook her head. "I was so mad at myself. These," she added, wriggling the fingers that held the rocks, "were not cheap, you know."

"What it is?" Lily asked, staring again at the blue rocks.

"Ah."

Lily glanced up. Margaret hadn't actually *blushed* per se, but she certainly seemed… abashed.

"Well. You see, it's her tenth birthday, double digits and all, a bit special, and she's been very interested in rocks and stones and geology since she was six, so, uh… They're sapphires."

Lily's eyes widened. "What, all of them?" she blurted. There were what, six, seven… eight. Eight rocks about the size of the tip of her pinky sitting there in Margaret's hand, and sure, they'd shrink down a lot if they were cut and polished, but holy moly.

Holy *cow* moly.

"It's rather extravagant, I know," Margaret murmured, gaze downcast. "You must understand"—she met Lily's eye very briefly—"I never had much growing up. My parents lived through the Great Depression, they both worked two jobs each to make ends meet. I just…"

Lily softened, offered Margaret a warm, gentle smile. "You just wanted your grandkids to have a better life than you did," she said.

"Yes." Margaret's expression turned grateful.

"I understand," said Lily.

"Thank you." Margaret's hand curled around the stone, and carefully, she let them drop out of her fist and back into the pouch. "I very much appreciate it."

One stone lingered between forefinger and thumb, catching was little light there was from the overcast sky, looking like a piece of the rainclouds had come down and solidified here in Margaret's hand.

Margaret stretched out the stone toward Lily. "I want you to have this."

"What? No, I can't possibly. That's far too much."

"Take it," Margaret said, lifting the uncut sapphire higher. "I insist. As you can see, I have no shortage here."

Lily swallowed, eyes on the stone. "Margaret. Really?" She searched Margaret's face, left eye, right eye, left again. "You can't." A whole sapphire? That was… Overwhelming. Too much.

"I can, and I insist," Margaret said. "Please." She nodded once, decisive. "You've saved me so much."

Lily stretched out her hand.

The stone landed in it, lightweight enough but holy cow, an entire sapphire the size of her pinky tip.

Margaret grinned. "It's worth about twenty-five dollars," she said, wrapping the loose strings of the pouch tightly around its mouth.

Some strange sort of relief drenched Lily's body; she realised her pulse had sped up, adrenalin zinging around her system at the prospect of the stone.

Twenty-five dollars.

She sagged a little against the door post. That was a much, much more reasonable reward for her efforts. "Thank you," she said, injecting as much of that into her tone as she could.

Margaret's smile, soft and broad and bright-eyed, said she understood. "You're more than welcome. Did your family find any mushrooms?"

Lily laughed. "Yes, we did, and my husband ate them and hasn't died yet, so I think we did okay."

Margaret nodded. "Well done. Your children are lucky to have parents like you."

A warm blush stole through Lily's chest. "And your grandkids are lucky to have you."

Margaret said goodbye, snapped open her umbrella against the rain, and Lily went back into the house, tucking the blue stone into the pocket of her jeans. Maybe she'd get it set into a pendant or something. It certainly wouldn't hurt to have a reminder of that one, perfect afternoon of silver-bright silence and space with her family in the midst of the chaos of the world.

ABOUT THE AUTHOR

AMY LAURENS is an Australian author of fantasy and science fiction for both adults and young adults. She also writes non-fiction books, often on various aspects of writing. Also dogs. Lots of dogs.

After completing a university education involving many twists and turns, through more faculties than ought reasonably to exist, Amy now spends her days as a high-school English teacher. No, she is not going to do your homework for you. Not even the English bit. Sorry. Have a cookie instead.

Amy has also written the award-winning portal-fantasy *Sanctuary* series about Edge, a 13-year-old girl forced to move to a small country town because of witness protection (the first book is *Where Shadows Rise*), the humorous fantasy *Kaditeos* series, following newly graduated Evil Overlord Mercury as she attempts to acquire a castle, the young adult series *Storm Foxes*, about love and magic and family in small town Australia, and a whole host of non-fiction.

Read more by Amy Laurens!

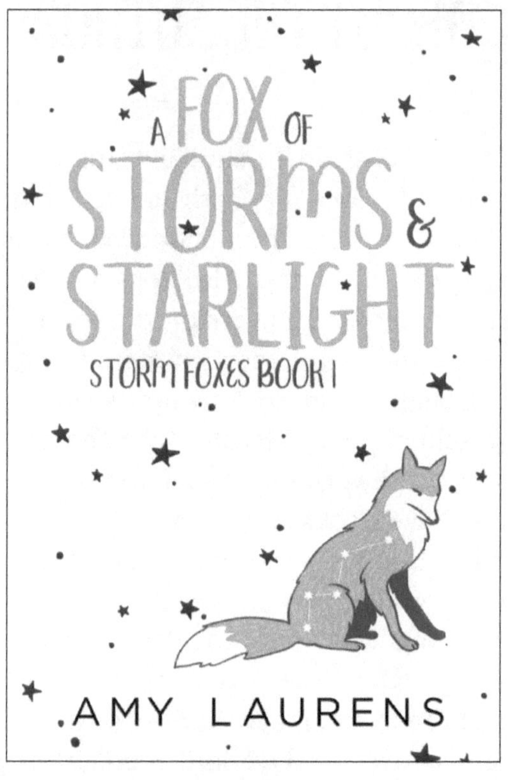

Chapter 1: Mina

SIX YEARS AGO, I SAVED a fox in the bush. It was only because my dog died. At the time, it felt like a pretty crappy bargain.

It was the first day of autumn—not by the calendar, but by the fresh bite in the morning air, the golden quality of the light as it lit the main road through town in the mid-afternoon.

Sailor was a big, black shaggy thing, something like a Newfoundland, a lively shadow in the golden light, and I was eleven.

I'm sorry to be starting any story this way, but the fact of the matter is, this where it all began.

I'll spare you the awful details. Enough to say that Sailor had got out of the yard somehow, and had been hit by a small-ish truck careening down the highway that split our tiny town in two as it blatantly ignored the speed limit.

I saw it happen.

And although I cradled him in my lap as the smell of burnt-out brakes and hot asphalt and turning leaves filled the air, his giant, furry black head all of him I could hold, there was nothing I could do.

There was nothing anyone could do.

I knew that, but it didn't stop the knot of frustration and guilt in my chest, or the taste of bile in the back of my throat every time I closed my eyes and saw the truck hitting him, again and again and again.

It took years for that vision to fade.

But that evening, only a few hours after it had happened, everything still felt fresh, and raw.

Sunny, my sister, was only nine at the time. She cried for hours, just sobbing like she'd never breathe right again.

I'd cried a little, at the scene with Sailor's head lying in my lap as one, brown eye stared up at nothing.

It had been mercifully fast, there was that.

And the driver had copped a massive fine—speeding, reckless driving, I think they even defected his truck—and came to visit us later, a big, pot-bellied man standing on our front verandah, shuffling his royal blue cap round and round and round in his hands as he apologised.

But that evening, with Sunny sobbing her heart out on the couch in the living room and Mum and Dad trying desperately to console her as dinner burned on the stove, I couldn't cry, even though the acrid scent of burning soy sauce, scorching brown sugar and smoking rice wine from the marinade prickled the back of my throat and the corners of my eyes.

I was the eldest, and I had to be responsible.

Possibly, if I'd been just a little more responsible, Sailor wouldn't have died.

So I slipped out the glass slider from the family room to the deck while Sunny cried, glancing up at the two storeys of our moody grey house behind me before jumping down from the rail-less deck to the lawn, and set out for the gate in the back fence.

I couldn't cry, and I didn't want to add anything to an already chaotic and stressful situation inside—but I couldn't stay there, either.

In the gaps between the gum trees to the west, the sky tinged to red and gold at the horizon, the sun sinking slowly into oblivion. I'm pretty sure I didn't know the word oblivion back then, but I knew what it meant, how it felt—and I craved it, desperately.

Anything would be better than the gaping hole in my chest.

And so, because I didn't know where to find it or how to get there, I stalked through the bush, pushing myself until I breathed hard and my lungs ached and sweat ringed me, chasing the way that hard exercise elevated me over my constantly looping thoughts.

Directly above, dark, heavy clouds obscured the sky, and the air was thick, heavy, humid.

Beneath the smell of dry gum leaves and even drier dirt, I could catch a hint of ozone, and occasionally the wind turned cool for a breath as it gusted against my skin, promising a late-evening storm.

I strode harder, faster, outpacing the video looping in my mind of the truck's impact.

When the first drops of rain spat at me from out of the sky, I barely noticed. My skin was filmed with sweat, slick and salty, and the peppering of rainwater barely added to it.

That was at first.

But within minutes, it became clear that those first pattering spits had been the early foreshadowing of a storm darker and more intense than any I remembered.

Thunder rolled across the sky, distant and grumbling at first, a lazy background chorus to the rhythmic melody of the rain as it splattered down on grey-green leaves and red-tinged twigs, turning the silvered bark of an old, dead gum to deep grey and making the spiky, tussocky grass seem oddly luminescent in the dying light.

I stood under a grey gum with stains down its trunk that the rain was turning orange, arms wrapped around myself, shivering hard—and for the briefest instant, thought about not going home.

Mum and Dad would pitch a fit.

And I had to be responsible.

I turned, dark t-shirt plastered to my skin, dark hair sticking to my face and clinging to my neck and began trudging my way back.

The storm closed over properly, clouds rolling over the horizon and cutting off the thin scythe of blood-coloured sunset, making the bush dark and unwelcoming in the premature night.

Lightning flashed.

Thunder cracked hot on its heels.

I jumped—and stared hard at the gap between two ghost-barked trees, where for a second, I was sure I'd seen a pair of eyes.

Nothing moved.

Nothing except the drenching rain, anyway, weighing down the branches that tossed fitfully in the wind.

My pulse slowly calmed.

There were rumours we'd all grown up with here in Jilamatang that spoke of something strange and dark… But that was in the forest north of here, in the pines, the plantation—not here, not in the natural, native bush.

I shivered.

The smell of wet dirt and soaked bark rose around me, undercut by eucalypt and ozone.

If anything had the power to wash away the hurt inside me, this storm was it. I tipped my face to the sky, imagining that the rain washing over me had the ability to wash me inside as well, and the raindrops splattered hard on my cheekbones, my chin, my tightly closed eyelids.

More lightning.

More thunder, cracking over the constant hiss of the falling rain.

And in the distance, something eerie, lifting the

hairs on the back of my neck: a strange kind of high-pitched yowl, a cry that rang with moonlight and distance, cutting straight through the noise of the storm.

Bolts of lightning streaked across the sky—one—two—three in the space of half a second, followed immediately by a growling crack of thunder so immense it vibrated in my chest.

I ducked down instinctively into a crouch.

There, in the corner of my eye…

I froze with my arms over my head.

The strange cries came again—and they were closer. I stared hard at the place, low to the ground, where I was sure I'd seen something small, maybe the size of a cat.

Flash. Growl.

Rain spitting down.

There. Right there. A small animal, pointy ears, light coloured chin and throat…

The strange, eerie cries came a third time, and my heart pounded fiercely. Whatever was making the noise, it was close. Really close.

The little creature across from me reacted too, flattening itself to the ground.

My jaw twitched.

My heart pounded.

My fingertips bit into my upper arms.

Stay? Go?

Run? Freeze?

The hairs on my neck prickled again and goose-bumps broke out all over me.

Cold dread formed a knot in my stomach.

Something was coming.

Something worse than the storm.

I had to get home.

I made it halfway to standing—and a series of strange, awful noises made me freeze again. They were sharp, clacking, squealing sounds, like someone knocking two echoing stones against each other, interspersed with high-pitched yowling...

And the creature in the darkness screamed.

I threw my back against the gumtree behind me, pressing hard against it.

My heart hammered.

I peered back and forth in the dark, eyes wide.

Rain drenched down, but my throat was dry.

My pulse pounded faster.

The little creature screamed again—and as lightning flashed, I saw it on its back, legs slashing wildly at the air as something attacked.

The awful, clacking-yowling noises sounded right in front of me.

I slapped my hands over my ears, gasping. Water ran down my face, into my mouth, my eyes.

It was hurting.

Whatever the small thing was, it was getting hurt, and I'd seen enough animals hurting today.

Something in my chest snapped.

I flung myself across the ground, leaping tussocks and a fallen branch before I crashed to my knees.

I crawled closer, desperate, gasping for oxygen through the heavy curtains of rain.

I couldn't see it. Where?

Somewhere here, near the base of that tree…

The yowling screeched right next to my ear. I cowered against the ground, spiky grass pricking my face, wet-earth smell smothering me—but now, there was a strange mustiness too, a cousin to wet-dog smell.

At the next flash of lightning, I saw it.

The creature was a fox—and something barely visible was attacking it, only the gleam of eye or flicker of teeth visible in the gloom.

But the damage was real enough.

The little fox's side had been opened right up, and in the bright, stark flashes of heavenly electricity, the blood was dark, thinned by the constant rain.

No.

No more animals were going to die today.

Not when this time, I could do something about it.

I snatched at a branch on the ground that turned out to be more of a glorified twig, and launched myself toward the creature.

I had no idea what was attacking it, but I screamed and waved my handful of twiggy leaves anyway, batting them in the air like I knew what I was doing.

The horrible clacking cries ceased abruptly.

With one long, low rumble, the rain began to ebb.

I poised, waiting.

But nothing came.

The attackers were gone.

Still gasping for air, pulse galloping in my throat, I sat next to the fox and shifted it carefully into my lap, realising as I tasted salt that I was crying.

I huddled over, trying to shelter the poor creature from the slackening rain, running my fingers over its wiry cheek—over and over and over and over.

"Please," I sobbed, throat tight and aching, chest constricted. "Please. Please don't die. Please."

Please, I prayed to anything that might be listening. *No more death. Not today.*

Not today.

Another gust of cool air washed over the clearing, taking the last of the rain with it—and lifting the goosebumps on my arms again.

And as it did, I could have sworn I heard a voice. *Neither do I wish him to die now.*

I shivered, drawing the fox close, like it was a stuffed animal I could hug for comfort—its comfort or mine, I couldn't say. I glanced around the dripping bush, eyes wide. The rumours spoke of an evil presence, and I could easily believe that might be what had attacked the fox.

But a voice? No one had ever mentioned a voice.

There was nothing to be seen, and anyway the

voice had sounded kindly—and didn't want the fox to die.

Assuming I hadn't just imagined it, of course. Which, half-drowned by grief, the other half drowned by the storm... An over-active imagination seemed highly likely.

Can you fix him? I thought it hard, though, just in case someone really was listening.

Something shifted in my lap.

Around us, the world stilled, dazed from the storm, but also something more, something watching, something waiting, as the bush held its collective breath.

The only sound was the occasional drip of rainwater from the gum leaves onto a fallen log—no insects, no wind, no rustling of leaves.

Just... stillness.

And the fox, who shivered in my lap.

The clouds tore open, revealing a ragged triangle of stars that glittered in the fox's eye as it blinked open and stared up at me.

My chest snagged.

My throat ached from crying, and a headache was forming in the back of my head.

But the fox blinked up at me—alive.

I ran a finger down it again, from nose to cheek to ear to shoulder, all the way down its side to its thick, bushy tail—and the wound in its side began to close.

Laboriously, it hauled itself to its front legs.

I tried to stop it—"No, it's okay, you can stay here, I'll look after you"—but it lifted its top lip to show half-hearted teeth, and staggered away.

As it did, I thought perhaps its fur began to shrink.

And suddenly, it looked larger in the night—as large as a dog, as large as Sailor…

But I blinked, and it was just a trick of the light, because the creature that darted away into the bushes like nothing was wrong at all was clearly a fox, the size of a large cat or maybe a small beagle, and nothing more.

And if something screamed in the night not long afterward, and the cry sounded horribly, horribly human?

Well.

I was halfway back toward home again by then, and I pressed my fingertips to my lower eyelids and prayed my parents wouldn't murder me for getting home so late.

Keep reading! Head to
<u>www.inkprintpress.com/amylaurens/ stormfoxes/</u>
to buy your copy now!

www.ingramcontent.com/pod-product-compliance
Lightning Source LLC
Chambersburg PA
CBHW050540190726
48284CB00003B/1149